A New Friend

The curtains in Tony's bedroom were twisting in the wind. Tony was just reaching for the window latch when he heard a wheezing nasal voice behind him.

"What clan are you from, brother?" the voice said.

Tony froze. Some stranger had gotten into his bedroom!

"Hello?" he said, his eyes searching every corner of the room.

He checked under his bed—nothing. What about the heavy oak wardrobe? Was the door moving? Had something crept in? Was it lurking in there, ready to pounce?

Tony peered into the cold, gloomy fireplace. Then he gasped when he saw the boy. He was about nine or ten, very pale with spiky black hair. He looked familiar to Tony.

It was the vampire boy from his dream!

The Little Vampire

A novelization by
Angela Sommer-Bodenburg
and
Nicholas Waller

Based on the screenplay by
Karey Kirkpatrick & Larry Wilson

Based on the children's book series
"The Little Vampire"
by Angela Sommer-Bodenburg

A MINSTREL® BOOK

Published by POCKET BOOKS
New York   London   Toronto   Sydney   Singapore

A MINSTREL PAPERBACK *Original*

A Minstrel Book published by
POCKET BOOKS, a division of Simon & Schuster, Inc.
1230 Avenue of the Americas, New York, NY 10020

ISBN: 0-7434-2145-0

First Minstrel Books printing October 2000

10   9   8   7   6   5   4   3   2   1

Book design by Arielle Rodriguez
Insert design by Jaime Putorti

Printed in the U.S.A.

Foreword

Do books need forewords? Not really. Does the book of the film *The Little Vampire* need a foreword? Not really, either. Or maybe it does.

Whatever the case, it is my wish to announce, before you read this book, how much I delight in the story told by the film. Larry Wilson and Karey Kirkpatrick created the screenplay from my novels about The Little Vampire. In doing so, they strayed in some points from the original plot. Yet I have absolutely no problem with that, and here is why. They have remained true to the spirit of my story. By spirit I do not mean any form of ghost, rather that which is at the heart of my books, namely: friendship, tolerance, understanding, solidarity, and the courage to be different, but also fun and adventure.

There is a rich vein of fun and adventure in the film! Some of the ideas developed by Larry and Karey are so good that I sometimes wish I had thought of them myself. But you will see for yourself.

To close, I would like to express my gratitude to Richard Claus, the producer of the film. He, like no other (excepting Burghardt Bodenburg), believed in *The Little Vampire* and in me, and it was he who made this film possible. A big vampire thank you also to Uli Edel, the director, who succeeded in bringing my little vampire to life in front of the camera.

Angela Sommer-Bodenburg

Chapter 1

Tony Thompson was having the weird vampire dream again.

It seemed so real, as though he was really there, floating in his bed, watching. And every time he had the dream the same thing happened.

It took place on a high cliff overlooking the ocean. A rising full moon seemed about to be hit by a comet. A tall, pale vampire with sad eyes stood on the cliff, staring out to sea, while over his head, on a long chain, he spun a humming circle of gold.

Summoned by the signal, other vampires flew in from all sides until thirty or forty or fifty were gathered on the cliff. They all wore strange old-fashioned clothes, like those in library books

1

about Shakespeare's time. There were a few children, some about Tony's age, which was eight.

When everyone seemed to have arrived, the leader stopped spinning and caught the gold object in his hand. It was a fabulous golden amulet on a chain that flashed with starlight. A curved outer section was engraved with strange symbols. Set into its center was a brilliant red jewel that glowed with hidden power.

As the comet approached the moon, a woman standing next to the leader turned and smiled, her sharp vampire teeth sparkling, and said, "Frederick, the clan is gathered, and it is time."

"Yes, Freda," said Frederick. "It is time." And the same simple ceremony unfolded.

Frederick took a deep breath and held the amulet up in the air. The moon turned red. A sizzling bright beam danced from the joined comet and the moon to bathe all the waiting vampires with red light the color of blood.

"*Ab ovo,*" Frederick intoned as the other vampires gazed blissfully toward the sky. "*Nil desperandum.*"

In Tony's dreams, every time Frederick got to that point, the same thing happened: the deep thumping of horses' hooves pounding the turf interrupted the ceremony.

All the vampires turned. The flaming torches of a fearsomely large wooden cart appeared out of the mist. Drawn by two huge horses whose hooves kicked up black clods of earth, the cart was heavily laden with antivampire weapons—bows and silver arrows, stakes and mallets and spades.

A massive bearded vampire hunter clothed in furs drove the frenzied horses on with terrible cries. A sinister necklace made from sharp fangs danced at his neck.

The hunter lifted a massive sword as he thundered closer.

"It's Rookery!" shouted Frederick. "Fly! Fly for the hills!"

Some of the other vampires scattered, rising into the air or transforming themselves into bats. Others, including one young boy, always stood their ground and bared their terrifying teeth in defiance.

"You must flee!" said Frederick as he stepped forward alone, toward the advancing threat.

Rookery bore down on Frederick, ignoring the boy and the others. He leaped from his cart, his eyes glinting with greed, his hands reaching out for the fabulous jewel.

Frederick held the amulet high as they fought, struggling backward and forward, forward and backward, and with one last great effort Rookery got a hand on his prize.

Spungg!!

The red stone burst out of its setting in the amulet and soared high in the air, twisting and glittering as it flew over the cliff edge. Frederick was left with just the golden outer section on its chain.

Usually at this point Tony woke up.

Tonight was different.

Suddenly he was floating just above the surface of the foaming, choppy sea as the jewel hit the water with a sizzling splash and disappeared toward the bottom, its red glow fading as it sank out of sight.

"Von!" came a shrieking cry from above. "Von, don't!"

Tony turned and looked up to the cliffs.

A dashing young vampire—Von—dived off the cliff, swooping after the stone, straight down toward Tony.

Eyes wide, cloak flapping, teeth bared, Von was going to crash right onto the bed!

Suddenly scared, Tony hid under the bed-clothes just in time.

Bang!

Tony sat bolt upright in the darkness, shouting. He felt sweaty and uncomfortable, his hair sticking straight up. What a nightmare!

Lightning flashed, followed by another loud bang. Rain tapped at the windows like bony fingers.

Tony turned on his bedside light and put on his glasses.

He was glad to find he really was in his own

bed in his own room, with his own teddy bear, and everything was as normal as it could be when you've just moved to a new house.

Suitcases and trunks were scattered around his room. Some of his stuff was already unpacked and spread about. Every day the place seemed a little more like home. Photos of his friends back in San Diego were mounted on the wall, next to a poster of Sammy Sosa. A signed football sat on the mantel alongside several robots that gleamed like protective guards.

Tony liked to remember the happy, sunny days in California, but they seemed far away now that he was living in a damp old castle in the middle of a storm in the cold wilds of Scotland.

The wind howled and rattled the window. Tony shivered. Maybe some ancient ghostie was trying to get in. Another flash of lightning cracked the sky, and the thunder seemed to burst right above his head.

That was it. He leaped out of bed and ran as fast as he could out the door and down the dark corridor to his parents' room, hoping that if he was quick enough no horrible thing would catch him with its cold hands and squeeze his neck.

"Waah!" he cried, pushing open his parents' door and rushing in. "Mom!" he shouted breathlessly.

Crash! He tripped over a huge bag of golf clubs and fell sprawling on the floor, sending the clubs clattering noisily.

Tony's mother, Dottie Thompson, sat straight up in bed. She shook her husband, Bob.

"Ryder Cup!" said Bob suddenly, woken from a dream.

Dottie shook him again. "I heard burglars!" she whispered loudly.

"Wuhh?" said Bob, his voice thick with sleep. Dottie turned on her bedside light. Their room, too, was full of boxes and half-unpacked suitcases.

"Only thunder," Bob mumbled.

A tousled little head appeared at the end of their bed, looking scared.

"Umm, hi, Mom," said Tony.

"Tony!" Dottie exclaimed. "What are you doing down there?"

"Mom, Dad, the vampires are back!"

"What?" said Bob.

"Was it another nightmare?" Dottie asked kindly, patting the bedcovers beside her. "Here, c'mon."

Tony gratefully trotted around to her side of the bed. "Mom, I think the house is haunted!"

"This is ridiculous. Do you know what time I have to get up?" Bob complained. "And I was just about to hit the winning putt, too."

Blearily he watched his son climb onto the bed. "Tony, you're too old to act like this."

Dottie put her arms around Tony encouragingly. "Don't worry, hon."

"Mom, do you like it here?" Tony asked her.

Bob sighed theatrically and turned his back on

them, puffing up his pillow loudly. Dottie briefly glared at him, stroking Tony's hair affectionately.

"It's a big change for you, I know," she said, turning off the light. "It's a new house, in a strange country. But a lot of kids would love the chance to live here."

Tony nestled in his mother's arms. He was just beginning to feel a bit safer from evil monsters when the wind whistled again.

"Hear that?" he said.

"Hush, now," said Dottie.

"It's just the wind," said Bob.

"Or the undead! They're in trouble!" Tony cried.

"Tony!" said Bob. "If I don't get some sleep, I will be one of the undead!"

"Dad's right," said Dottie. "Try to sleep now, hon."

"Yeah. And no more dreaming!"

But Tony couldn't sleep. He stared into space, thinking.

Why was he always dreaming of vampires?

Chapter 2

In the morning the rain stopped.

Bob had already gone to work by the time Dottie managed to get Tony up and dressed in his school outfit, though it was a struggle. Tony was in no hurry. He dawdled over his cornflakes, hoping to make his mother think it was a Saturday or something. No such luck.

"Hurry up, hon, or you'll be late," she said.

"That's fine by me," muttered Tony.

"What was that?"

"Sorry, Mom, be right on it." Tony sighed and dragged his book bag through the hall.

"Hey, why the long face?" Dottie asked, smiling brightly and locking the front door. "You love school."

Tony stepped over a large puddle in the driveway and clambered into the car without answering.

Dottie glanced at him worriedly as she started the car. Tony looked morosely out the window at his new home as he buckled his seat belt. He tried to convince himself that what his mom had told him last night was right.

Just look at the place, he told himself. Lots of kids would love to live in a real castle. True, it was only a small castle, and a lot had been changed over the years to make it into a modern home. Still, it looked great—it had thick stone walls and fortified turrets. There were big trees in the garden, and hedges and ivy-covered walls and pathways on different levels. Tony even had his very own room at the top of a tower, like the ones damsels with very long hair had to live in when they were in distress.

Nearby was a genuine lord's stately home, where Tony's dad worked, and a big old ruined church and a pretty village and rolling countryside and even an ocean. Though not as big as the Pacific, it was still pretty impressive. But this new place did not feel like home.

"Scotland is beautiful, isn't it?" said Dottie as she pulled out of the driveway and straight onto the right-hand side of the road leading into the town of Dindeen. The sunlight sparkled in the lush grass, which was soaked from the previous night's storm.

"It's too wet," said Tony, mentioning just one main difference between Scotland and home.

"Well, I like the way the sun shines through gaps in the clouds every once in a while," said Dottie happily. "Very dramatic. And we do get a lot of great rainbows."

Tony glanced at her and smiled. "Always look on the bright side, huh?" he said. "I guess no one gets thirsty."

"Look, hon," Dottie said, more seriously, "it's certainly not California, but I do like the fact that we're out of the city, in the countryside with the fresh air and the farm animals."

She waved vaguely at a herd of black-and-white Friesian cows as they passed a field on their neighbor Farmer McLaughlin's land. Up ahead on the road, a little red tractor trundled toward them. There was something strange about that tractor, thought Tony, but he couldn't put his finger on what.

"And I know school's different, but you'll soon get used to the way they do things here," said Dottie. "The TV, school, the money, and—"

The man on the tractor shouted angrily at them. Tony realized what was wrong.

"You're driving on the wrong side of the road, Mom!" he yelled.

Dottie spun the steering wheel, and the car swerved hard to the left, just avoiding an accident. The tractor driver, old Farmer McLaughlin himself, shook his fist at them as they drove on, shouting something that sounded like "Sassenach loons."

"And they talk funny, too," said Tony.

Dottie laughed. "Better not tell your dad about that little incident," she said as they drove down the hill toward McAshton Manor. "And here he comes now."

"Where?" said Tony.

"See if you can spot him."

Tony stared out of the window. Lord McAshton's place was a hive of activity. Workers in hard hats were carrying scaffolding and lumber, big trucks were delivering mysterious things, earthmovers were scouring the landscape. Tony knew his dad had something important to do with the project that was advertised on the huge billboard beside the road—McAshton Manor Convention Centre and Golf Club—but he could never figure out exactly what. Perhaps everything.

"I see him!" he shouted.

"Where?"

"There!" Tony pointed. Bob was standing by his Land Rover, talking to a man on a big black horse. Immediately Tony thought of the horses in his dream, and shivered.

"That's Lord McAshton himself," said Dottie.

The two men seemed to be discussing a gigantic floppy gray sheet spread out across the ground. It looked like a flattened whale. Ripples of air ran through it.

"Hey!" said Tony. "Is that the blimp?"

"Sure is." Dottie beeped the horn twice. Bob and Lord McAshton looked up. "Wave, hon."

"He won't see me," said Tony, but he waved anyway.

"Yup, that big ol' blimp is going to fly today." Dottie sat back as they left McAshton Manor behind. "We're going to a party for its launch tonight."

"Oh," said Tony sullenly. "I guess I'm not invited."

"Don't be like that. Plenty of boring adult talk, I expect. You won't miss much." She sighed. "C'mon, hon. This is such a great opportunity for Dad. It should be a great adventure for you. Just you wait! You'll soon settle down and make friends at school."

Tony slumped in his seat, reminded again of school. Although it was a sunny day, a dark cloud settled over his face.

Chapter 3

Tony walked reluctantly through the gates of the school playground and almost immediately found himself at the center of a crowd of happy, laughing children all much taller than he was.

Unfortunately, they were laughing at him, not with him.

"What are you still doing here, Yank?" said Nigel McAshton, a hard-faced, short-haired boy, as he looked down at Tony. "Didn't we tell you to go home?"

"Aye, we don't want your sort here," said Flint, his squinty-eyed brother.

"But it's not my fault!" Tony protested. "I didn't want to come here!"

"Not good enough for you, eh?" Nigel hit him in the stomach, hard.

"Oof!" Tony bent over, winded and unable to speak.

"That's for being a little creep," said Nigel.

His brother, meanwhile, got down on all fours and crawled behind Tony. Nigel pushed Tony backward over Flint, and Tony landed heavily, dropping his book bag.

"And that's for coming here in the first place!"

Tony's glasses fell off into the grass. All the other kids howled with laughter.

Flint stood up, holding Tony's bag.

"What have we got here?" he asked. "Let's see." He turned the bag over, dumping out its contents.

Books and pens and Tony's lunch fell out into a mud puddle. His apple rolled toward Nigel, who squashed it into the ground.

"Teacher won't be happy, Yank," he said. "You coming to school all dirty like that."

The bell rang, sending the kids scurrying inside. Tony put his glasses back on and watched them go into the gloomy gray stone building. He was as miserable as he'd ever been in his short life.

"Mom," he said to himself. "What was wrong with San Diego anyway?"

🦇

Ten minutes after that, Tony could hardly believe his eyes and ears.

Mr. Boggins, his teacher, was drawing on the blackboard—drawing a comet crossing the moon, just as in Tony's dream! What was going on? How did he know about that?

Tony sat there in amazement, forgetting for the moment that he was in between the twin terrors, Nigel and Flint.

"Do close your mouth, Tony Thompson," said Mr. Boggins, "or you'll swallow a midgie. And wipe the mud off the end of your nose, there's a good lad."

The other kids tittered. Tony blushed as he scrubbed at his nose with a handkerchief.

Mr. Boggins pointed at his drawing. "What's that?"

Nigel and Flint fiercely surveyed the classroom. They didn't know the answer, so no one else could know. All the other children shifted uneasily in their seats, unwilling to show up the ignorant bullies. Tony also kept his mouth shut, because he had been told to.

"It's a comet. Comet Forsey," said Mr. Boggins. "And we're in for a real treat. On Saturday night we'll be able to see Comet Forsey in conjunction with the moon for the first time in three hundred years. And then—"

"And then," said Tony, unable to contain himself, "there's a big beam of lightning and the moon goes bright red, like blood!"

His classmates turned to look at him.

"What on earth makes you say that?" said Mr. Boggins.

"It's like in my dream!"

Nigel and Flint looked at each other and snorted dismissively. A few of the other kids sniggered.

"Quiet!" said Mr. Boggins.

"It's been in my dream every night since I've been here," said Tony.

"Stupid Yank!" Nigel said under his breath.

"And there's a gathering."

"A gathering? A gathering of what?" Mr. Boggins asked.

"Of vampires."

"Oh, no, Tony, not again!" said Mr. Boggins, raising his eyes to the ceiling. Everyone laughed out loud.

"But I really saw it! The comet, the moon, the big fangs—"

"Tony!"

"And there's a vampire hunter! He's big and hairy with horses and a cross—"

The whole class was in an uproar.

"Tony," said Mr. Boggins, pointing at the door, "I've warned you before. You've earned yourself a visit to the headmistress."

Tony walked out of the room, blushing deeply, listening to the jeers and catcalls of his class-mates.

"But I did see them!" he muttered to himself. "And the horses and the jewel and everything!"

Chapter 4

*L*ater that same day, Tony sat alone in his bedroom, drawing.

He usually didn't draw unless he was told to at school for art, but now he was working hard on a whole series of scenes from his dreams. He stuck his tongue out as he worked. He was concentrating so hard on coloring some of the smaller jewels on a picture of the weird amulet that he did not hear his father open the door.

Clunk!

A golf ball banged into the table leg. Tony looked around, surprised. His dad stood there in the doorway, dressed in a smart tuxedo and holding up a small golf club.

"Hi, Dad," said Tony.

"Hi, Tony," said Bob. "Look what I got you." From behind his back he produced a golf bag full of small clubs.

"Golf clubs?" said Tony, taken aback.

"A junior set, just for you. Did you know golf was invented in Scotland?"

"You have mentioned it before," said Tony. He felt miserable. "But I don't have anyone to play with."

"That's the beauty of the game," said Bob, taking another swish with the club and gazing off into space. "You don't need anyone to play with. Just you and the open landscape and the fresh air."

"But I want someone to play with."

"Well, I'll play with you. I'll teach you."

"You never have time!"

"I'll make time."

"That's what you said about skiing in San Diego."

Bob's eyes narrowed. "I'm trying here, Tony! I promise."

"Sorry, Dad. Okay! Let's play right now!"

Bob's face fell. "Oh, well, not right now, Tony." He pointed at his black tie.

"Why," said Tony innocently, "are you going somewhere?"

"We've got to go out. Sorry."

"Oh, okay, whatever." Tony turned back to his drawings.

Behind him, Bob looked up at the ceiling and made a face. "It's important, Tony. Business. Lord McAshton's invited us to dinner up at the manor. Everyone will be there."

"Uh-huh," said Tony, his attention on the intricate pattern around the edge of the amulet. "Not me, though."

Dottie came in, wearing a black dress and struggling with her earrings. Bob glanced at her and shrugged, as if to say, I tried.

"Lorna's arrived," she said. Tony looked up. "Lorna's your baby-sitter, hon."

"When will you be back?" Tony asked.

"Not too late. Sorry, baby," she said, giving him a big hug.

"Mom!" he said. "I keep telling you I'm not a baby!"

"Oh, sorry, hon. I keep forgetting." She picked up Tony's drawing. "Hey, I'm impressed. I didn't know you could draw this well."

Tony looked at his artwork with a critical eye. The drawings really were pretty good.

"Well, you know, Mom, neither did I," he said, puzzled. "It all just sort of came out of me."

Bob picked up a sheet. "Oh, no!" he said, showing Dottie a fearsome vampire, complete with cape, huge sharp teeth, and staring red eyes.

"It's very well done," said Dottie, treading carefully.

"Right, great," said Bob as he tossed the drawing down. "All vampires and monsters! No wonder everyone thinks you're a crazy freak!" He looked at Tony sternly. "If you want to do something really cool, draw me a picture of Tiger Woods." With that he turned on his heel and walked out.

Tony looked up at his mother, startled.

"He's a little . . . tense, I guess, Tony," said Dottie. "You're no crazy freak. But this is an important week for Dad. Some big decisions at work." She bit her lip thoughtfully. "It would help if . . . if he didn't have to worry about you and your obsession. Try to think about that."

"But it's not an obsession—"

"Tony!"

"Okay, Mom," said Tony. "I'll try."

At about the same time, in another part of the countryside surrounding the village, a loud growl shattered the silence just as the sun set. An enormous modified tow truck, solid and red, a hefty roaring beast of a machine, eased over a hill overlooking the village and pulled to a stop, throbbing and rattling with power. Mud was caked in the deep treads of its heavy black tires.

The truck looked as if it had just come out of a war and was ready to go into another one, which in a sense it was. It was laden with all sorts of equipment—a drill, a searchlight, deep-sea fishing gear, a rocket launcher for wooden stakes, strings of garlic, crosses and crossbows, lamps and spades and pickaxes and a sledgehammer.

Inside the cab the driver lit a fat cigar, took a draw, and smiled broadly. If Tony had seen him, he would have recognized him. The driver had no full beard now, just stubble, and his clothes were modern: a leather jacket and heavy trousers, studded with skulls and feathers. Around his neck was a garland of sharp fangs—vampire fangs.

He looked like the vampire hunter in Tony's dream—exactly like him!

Bob and Dottie got out of their Land Rover and looked around them.

"Hey, this is great," said Bob, handing his keys to a polite young man who got in and drove away. "They really did a good job of tidying up."

"You're sure they have valet parking in Scotland?" Dottie asked as she watched their car disappear into darkness.

McAshton Manor did look great, big and wealthy and solid. High above it a banner bearing the McAshton coat of arms fluttered proudly in a light breeze. All the windows on every floor of the mansion glowed a friendly golden color from the blazing chandeliers inside. Huge candles led the way from the gravel driveway to where a kilted piper stood at the massive entrance door, his bagpipes welcoming the guests with loud skirls and wails.

Beside him stood Lord McAshton, tall and resplendent in his own kilt, peering at his guests through a monocle. His thinning gray hair was blown about by the breeze. Dottie couldn't help noticing his eyebrows, which must have been specially brushed and now looked like fat caterpillars.

"Ahh, so glad you could come, Bob, Dodie," he said, beaming proudly.

"Dottie, Lord McAshton," said Dottie.

"Dottie? Of course you are!" He winked. "Umm. Your blimp thingy looks quite marvelous, don't you think?"

Bob and Dottie turned to follow his gaze. High above them the blimp, fully inflated now, floated like a big whale in the sky, proclaiming the convention center and golf course to the world, or at least that part of it that happened to drive past the entrance.

"I—" said Dottie.

"My great-great-grand . . ." McAshton furrowed his brow. "Someone or other knew the Montgolfiers, you know."

The piper squawked a particularly loud squeak. Dottie winced.

"I like your bagpipes," Bob said quickly.

McAshton smiled. "They have a proper rhythm, haven't they? That's what so much of this modern music lacks. Any rhythm."

"Perhaps we could have a piper greet all the golfers on the first tee?" Bob suggested.

"Oh, yes, just the thing to relax them," said Dottie.

"Capital! This is why I fought so hard to bring Bob over," McAshton said. "He's always bursting full of ideas! He has vision!" He leaned toward Dottie conspiratorially. "We'll be able to leverage our position here to maximize revenue stream with his revolutionary marketing proposals."

"That's great," said Dottie, smiling. Bob ushered her indoors.

"What kind of golfers are mont golfers?" he asked.

"I have no idea. He forgot my name again, Booby."

"At least he—"

"Liked your blimp. I know."

🦇

In his bedroom Tony put his pile of drawings to one side and began experimenting with the vampire look. If you can't beat them, join them, he reasoned. He put on a vampire cape from an old Halloween costume that his parents had not yet thrown away.

With his penknife he carefully cut a pair of big vampire fangs from white cardboard and tucked them under his upper lip.

He inspected the result in his mirror. Not bad. What did vampires do to look scary? He lifted one caped arm in front of his face. He frowned and opened his mouth wide and hissed loudly at his own reflection. Of course, *real* vampires couldn't be seen in mirrors.

There was a quick knock, and the door opened. The baby-sitter! Before Tony could move, Lorna saw him and jumped back in shock.

"Och! Laddie!" she said, one hand fluttering to her mouth. "You fair near stopped ma heart, and it's close enough to stoppin' as it is!" Recovering quickly, she smiled as she pulled the sheets back on Tony's bed and plumped up the pillows. "And you wouldn't want to do that to nice Miss Lorna, would you?"

She put her hands on her hips and looked down at Tony with mock severity.

"Now, you clean your teeth—all of them, mind, even the pointy ones—and off to bed wi' ya."

And with that she swirled out.

Tony grimaced at the closed door. "Bed—for the undead? Ha-ha-ha! I don't think so!"

Chapter 5

Far across the dark fields, a single small vampire bat fluttered through the air. A bat expert watching would have said the bat was exhausted, as if he had been on a very long journey and badly needed rest.

The bat passed in front of the fat yellow moon and flitted thankfully down toward its target—an ancient cemetery set in the grounds of a ruined church. Old columns wreathed in ivy stood like broken teeth in the moonlight. Crumbling walls hid nests of squeaking mice. Small bushes and trees pushed their gnarled, winding roots through the abandoned graves and paths. Mist drifted in layers through the chill air, like slow-moving ghosts lost on their way home.

No sensible human would have dared to go in there at that time of night. The caretaker himself rarely ventured in, preferring to stay indoors at the rectory, a rambling old house a couple of hundred yards away with a For Sale sign outside it.

The little bat fluttered across the abandoned nave and landed on a ruined arch, breathing fast. He looked around with beady black eyes. His nose twitched as he sampled the air.

Then suddenly a blast of light burst from nowhere. A searchlight! Its beam swung wildly around, piercing the mist and darting over stones and walls and pillars and crosses. The blinding white light sent stabbing fingers into every nook and cranny and found the bat cowering in an alcove, its wings over its eyes.

The bat had no choice. He squeaked and dropped off his perch, a tumbling tangled ball of fur and feet and teeth, and landed in the cool shadow behind a tombstone. He unfolded his wings, ducking to avoid the light, desperately seeking a way out. The cruel circle of light followed hard, cutting and thrusting.

Sitting in the cab of his truck, directing the beam, was Rookery, a cigar clamped in his grinning mouth, his piggy eyes narrowed in concentration, trying to follow the maddeningly twisting little shape as it curved and banked.

"So you think you're getting away, eh?" he said. "We'll see about that!"

He flicked a switch. On top of the truck a large wire dish device came to life and started swinging about, searching like a radar. In the cab, Rookery glanced at a flickering screen on his dashboard. The screen was part of the bat-locating system. "Come on!" he said, hitting it once, hard. It burst into orange life. A tiny white dot danced across it, moving away, out of the computerized map of the cemetery.

"Got you now, you filthy thing! Let the chase begin!"

With a noisy grinding of heavy cogs he put his big truck in gear and pulled out, glancing at the bat-locator screen from time to time as he bounced down the track and out onto the road.

The bat had a hard time staying in the air, let alone ahead of Rookery, but he flapped and flapped his wings, until he thought his heart would burst if he couldn't get some rest. But always behind him there was the roar of the truck, like a tidal wave coming to crash over him, steadily getting closer and closer.

Rookery stood on the accelerator. Smoke poured from the engine exhaust and the smoke-screen generator as the monster machine careened down tree-lined lanes in pursuit, its lamps blazing all around it like a mad Christmas tree. Rookery had one hand on the steering wheel, and with the other he swung the searchlight around, keeping the fluttering bat in his sights as much as possible.

Panting and weaving erratically from side to side, the bat fought to escape the harsh beam, dodging into the shadows when he could. There was nowhere to hide; he always had to keep flying. If he stopped, Rookery would catch him and that would be that—the end.

He couldn't outrun Rookery, but perhaps he could outsmart him. He saw a chance ahead—a gap in the trees, a gate into a field.

The bat turned sharply and fluttered over the gate, then banked hard to the left, flying alongside the hedge as low as he dared, out of sight.

Rookery, surprised, spat out his cigar. He spun the wheel hard and followed, smashing straight through the gate. Splintered planks flew high into the air. One hit the dish of the bat locator, snapping it off. The truck hit a water trough, sending up a great splash of water.

The truck skidded through the field. Cursing, Rookery spun the wheel again. Slipping and sliding, engine screeching and wheels spinning, the big truck turned around and slowly sank up to its axle in mud.

Rookery wouldn't be stuck for long, though, because he had a winch and all the other equipment he needed to pull himself out. But he was losing time.

Breathing deeply, he checked the bat-locator

screen. It was dark. He tapped it once or twice, then hit it hard with his fist, which made him feel better but did no good.

Muttering to himself, Rookery sent the searchlight beam scanning the darkness.

The bat flew on through the cool night air, dipping and weaving. He was almost ready to drop from exhaustion, but he had to take advantage of Rookery's accident. He had to get as far away as possible.

The distant searchlight beam hit him briefly, then passed on, lighting up a large house—a house built on the ruins of an old castle. A single light was on in the tower: Tony's house and Tony's bedroom. The beam paused, then moved on, scanning the sky.

Normally the bat would have avoided human houses, but this was an emergency. He fluttered over the lawn, over the rosebushes, over the driveway and Dottie's car, and up past the tower. His plan was to bank around the tower, then fly on into the darkness, protected from Rookery by the castle's shadow, and so make his escape.

But something made him pull up sharp in the air and hover there like a hummingbird, fluttering in astonishment.

Inside the tower room he could see a vampire! And what was more, he had trapped some food!

Chapter 6

Tony stalked across the room, holding his cape high, his cardboard teeth bared at his victim—his teddy bear, sprawled helpless on the bed.

A soft tap at the window made him jump, the hairs on the back of his neck rising. He looked around but saw nothing. Outside the window was only the blackness of the night, though he could hear the strange growl of an engine.

Tony turned back to the job at hand. Teddy lay on the bed, his neck exposed. Tony leaned forward.

A beam of pure white light from Rookery's searchlight blasted through the window, casting an enormous bat shadow on the wall. Tony spun around, terrified, clutching his bear, only to find himself blinded as the light shone straight into his eyes. The beam passed almost immediately, leaving Tony blinking away the dancing after-images. What was going on? He could hardly see.

As his vision returned, he noticed that, oddly, the window seemed to be wide open now.

The filmy curtains were twisting in the wind. Tony shivered. He was just reaching for the window latch when he heard a wheezing nasal voice behind him.

"What clan are you from, brother?" it said.

Tony froze. Some stranger had gotten into his bedroom!

"Hello?" he said, slowly moving away from the window, his eyes searching every corner of the room. He knelt suddenly and checked under his bed—nothing. He edged nervously toward the middle of the room. What about the heavy oak wardrobe? Was the door moving? Had something crept in? Was it lurking in there, ready to pounce?

Tony wondered if he should run to get Lorna.

There! He spotted some movement on the hearth. The iron stand with fireplace tools on it—the poker and the brush were swinging just slightly.

Tony peered into the gloom beyond, to the back of the cold fireplace. Then he gasped.

He saw a boy, about nine or ten, very pale with spiky jet-black hair, dressed in weird old-fashioned clothes—purple trousers, a tight-waisted jacket, tall leather boots. And he looked familiar. . . .

It was the defiant little vampire boy from his dream!

Except now he had a strange-looking nose, like a mouse. Or a bat. Tony stopped and thought about all this for a moment. Had he gone to sleep without realizing it? Was he dreaming again right now?

"Has the searchlight gone?" the vampire asked in a squeak. He seemed startled by the sound of his voice. Cross-eyed, he noticed his nose.

"Oh, no! I'm only half transformed again!"

He banged the side of his head with his hand. *Pop!* His nose popped into a proper human shape, and his transformation was complete.

Tony was so surprised at this that his mouth dropped open and his vampire fangs fell out.

"Who are you?" he said. "Are you a real vampire?"

The vampire looked up weakly and noticed Tony's teeth fluttering to the floor. He gasped, "You're not a brother!"

"I'm not a sister," said Tony.

"You're a human!" The little vampire's teeth chattered. "You're full of real blood!" he said, shuddering with the pain of an ancient longing.

"And I'm gonna keep it that way!" said Tony, backing away cautiously. Suddenly he turned and ran for the door.

Zzzzp!

With the speed of a bullet, the vampire was in front of him, hanging upside down in the doorway and blocking the exit. "I'm sorry," he said weakly. "I can't allow you to leave."

Tony stopped dead, unsure what to do next.

Then, slowly, the vampire slipped off the doorframe and crumpled headfirst onto the floor, landing on his back, groaning.

Tony could hear him muttering softly. It sounded like "Mustn't . . . mustn't bite him. Mustn't bite him. It's wrong. Got to get away. Mustn't bite him," over and over again.

His curiosity overcoming his fear, Tony crept forward and squatted beside the barely conscious little vampire. His eyes glittered like crystals of coal and he curled up in fear, his pale hands closing over his heart as if protecting himself from an expected attack.

But no attack came.

"Do you need help?" asked Tony.

"Help?" The little vampire looked at him through narrowed suspicious eyes. "What twisted kind of human are you?" He struggled to sit up, summoning his remaining reserves of energy.

Tony rocked back on his heels, still cautious. "I saw you in my dreams," he said.

"Must have been a nightmare," the vampire answered.

"It was," Tony replied.

"I must leave," the vampire said suddenly. He sprang to his feet, ran across the room, and dived straight out of the window, aiming to soar upward into the air and make his escape—but with no luck. Immediately he fell out of view, plummeting toward the ground, his arms and legs flailing like the blades of a windmill.

Tony ran to the window and looked down, to see his mysterious visitor spread-eagled on the grass twenty feet below. He looked so helpless that Tony knew he had to do something.

He turned off his bedroom lights and went out into the corridor. Carefully he crept along the wooden corridor and down the stairs, wincing at every sound. If Lorna saw him, he would be sent straight back to bed with a big Scottish flea buzzing in his ears.

Cautiously, he peeked into the living room. Lorna was there all right, staring blankly at the Thompsons' large TV, absentmindedly stuffing potato chips into her cavernous mouth. Luckily the old film she was watching had reached a particularly tense moment. Robin Hood was sneaking up on the Sheriff of Nottingham, or something like that.

Tony eased the front door open, stepped outside, and closed it softly behind him. Then he mentally slapped his head. He had locked himself out! Oh, well, he would worry about that later.

It was not too cool outside, which was just as well, as he was wearing only shorts and a T-shirt. He trotted around the corner to where the little vampire had landed. He seemed to be stirring.

"Are you all right?" Tony asked.

The vampire snorted as he painfully propped himself up on his arms. "Do I look all right?" he said in a weak voice. He shook his head to clear it.

Another burst of bright light shone out, this time from the main road. Tony could hear an engine growling.

"Oh, no!" said the vampire. "He's after me!"

Rookery had gotten his truck out of the muddy field and was back on vampire patrol, his searchlight again carving a path through the sky on its ceaseless hunt. The vampire struggled to move into cover, but he was too drained. Tony dragged him under the bushes. From that relative safety they watched the truck thunder by on the main road, steaming like a railway train.

"Who is that?" Tony whispered.

"Rookery," said the little vampire.

The name sounded familiar to Tony.

"He's the fiercest vampire hunter of them all! He's always after us."

Suddenly the vampire slumped to the ground again, his breath coming in short, sharp bursts.

"I'll help you get away," said Tony.

Painfully the vampire turned his head and looked up at Tony. He seemed to decide that he had no choice but to trust this strange human.

"Do you know," he said, breathing in short, sharp bursts, "where I can find a cow?"

"A cow?" said Tony, puzzled. "Well, if you want a glass of milk I—"

"Not milk," said the vampire, his eyes closing as he seemed to slip away into sleep. "A cow."

Tony furrowed his brow in thought.

Chapter 7

Five minutes later Tony was dragging the little vampire across Farmer McLaughlin's field in his wagon. It was hard work, pulling the wagon through the long grass and the mud puddles and around the cowpats and over the deep ruts dug by McLaughlin's tractor.

The little vampire—barely conscious, slumped over with his head between his knees—was no help at all. He was heavy, and Tony really had to struggle. All the while he kept an eye open for the big truck, but from what he could see of a bright jangle of lights moving slowly through the woods, Rookery seemed to be a mile or so away, perhaps led astray by an owl.

On the horizon, the dark hulking shape of

Farmer McLaughlin's barn was silhouetted against the sky. Tony didn't go out much after dark, and when he did it was usually in a car. He was surprised at how much he could see. Of course, the moon was getting brighter and brighter. In only a few days, according to Mr. Boggins, the moon would be full. Even now Tony could easily tell what was grass and what was track, what was hedge and tree and fence.

Finally they made it to the barn door.

"Here you are," said Tony, breathing hard but pleased with himself. "Cows." He pushed open the creaking old door. The warm, rich smell of living animals wafted out.

Inside five big black-and-white cows gazed at the boys with a dumb lack of interest, steadily munching hay from their ramshackle wooden troughs. They looked like they could be Lorna's sisters. Tony giggled to himself.

"Thank you," said the vampire, looking at him strangely.

"What now?" Tony asked as he helped the vampire clamber out of the wagon.

"First, I have to hypnotize one of them."

"Hypnotize! Wow!" The cows seemed pretty hypnotized already. "What for?"

"Otherwise they might call out and warn the mortals we are here. Now, please, no more questions. I don't have much time."

The vampire selected a big cow called Mitsy,

according to her ear tag. Tony watched fascinated as the vampire passed his hands in front of her face in a complex, fluid pattern that Tony couldn't follow—the vampire suddenly seemed to have seven hands!

Mitsy was confused almost instantly. She stopped chewing, and loose bits of hay fell out of her slack, drooling mouth. Her huge soft brown eyes tried to track the vampire's fingers, but they failed. Her eyelids drooped, and she was off, wandering the dark uplands of cow dreamland.

"Now what?" asked Tony.

By way of answer, the little vampire stepped around to the side of the cow, stroked her neck, then opened his mouth. His vampire fangs noticeably extended—and bit down hard! He closed his eyes in pleasure as he drank the warm blood.

"Uuuurgh! Gross!" said Tony.

The vampire looked up, puzzled, wiping his mouth. "Why? You eat beef, don't you?"

"That's not the same!"

"Why not?"

"We cook the beef first!"

"Urghh! So it's all dry and shriveled up."

Tony did not want to continue the argument. He knew what the vampire had done wasn't the same as eating beef, and he didn't want to watch anymore. If he did, he thought he might be sick.

"I'll just wait outside," he said, "until you're . . . until you're all done."

He turned and ran, one hand covering his mouth. He ran as far as the road, until the sound of slurping faded. He took a few deep breaths and felt better.

He stood there for a quiet moment, looking up at the stars and at the hills silhouetted against the sky. It was quiet but not completely quiet. There was a sound of gentle hissing from somewhere, probably some piece of farm machinery.

As Tony looked around, though, he became aware of a huge dark shape on the road about a hundred yards up the hill. It was not a house or a hut, as he first thought. Smoke seemed to be drifting from it. Tony screwed up his eyes and squinted into the darkness. The huge shape seemed to have four big fat wheels.

Suddenly a barrage of lights flared at him.

He raised his arm to shade his eyes. Rookery again! And with a roar like the biggest dragon you've ever heard, Rookery's truck started rolling down the road toward him, gaining speed.

In the cab Rookery grinned. "Oh, it's only a tiddler . . . Never mind! Got you now, you little bloodsucker!"

Tony turned and ran for his life as the truck accelerated, but he was only a little boy with short legs, and the truck was an enormously heavy machine going downhill. He couldn't possibly outrun it.

He began to panic. How could he escape?

It was gaining, closer, faster . . .

Whoosh!

Tony wasn't sure what happened next. There was a rush of wind, and he was hit from the side by a blur that pushed him out of the way.

As he fainted, Tony had the strangest feeling he was falling—but falling upward! He didn't hit the ground; he seemed to be falling into the clouds.

Rookery braked his massive vehicle to a halt.

He stood up on his driver's seat and popped his head through the hatch to look up at the sky. He turned his searchlight around uselessly.

"You can fly, but you can't hide!" he shouted. Frustrated, he pulled out his big black crossbow and fired an iron bolt. It went whizzing into the darkness and was lost forever.

Chapter 8

The big party at McAshton Manor was in full swing. A string quartet dressed in Highland costume played Scottish airs. Elegantly dressed guests in tuxedos and flouncy colorful ball gowns looked one another up and down, checking for serious social errors and whispering and sniggering whenever they saw one.

Dottie felt vulnerable to their snobbish gazes and whispers. Perhaps the other guests were envious that she and Bob, mere outsiders, stood with two of the highest pillars of local society, Lord McAshton and the Reverend Mr. Penhaligon, who was nearing the end of a long and pointless golfing story. "So on the fifteenth," he said, "a short par three with two bunkers on the left and four . . . no, five—or is it four? I think it's four. Or five. On the right. Say four, for argument's sake. And Buffy says to Monty, don't worry . . ."

Bob was nodding eagerly, but Dottie's eyes were glazing over. She had never liked golf, though she hid that fact from Bob as much as she could.

A small voice piped up from somewhere around her knees.

"Canapé, missus?" She glanced down to see two angelic-looking young boys holding up small trays of food.

"Ahh!" Lord McAshton said proudly, interrupting the vicar. "These chaps are my grandsons. Nigel and Flint, let me introduce you to Mr. and Mrs. Thompson, Tommy's parents."

Dottie glanced at Bob with raised eyebrows. "That's Tony," she said, then turned back to the boys. "How do you do?"

"My boys tell me that they've become great friends with your son," McAshton said, beaming.

"He's our favorite plaything," said Nigel.

"Playmate," corrected Flint.

McAshton looked at his watch. "I say, isn't it time you two young men were in bed?"

Nigel bowed to Dottie and smiled as if butter would not melt in his mouth. "Lovely to meet you, Mrs. Thompson. Tell Tony we look forward to seeing him tomorrow."

"Bright and early!" said Flint, and they both left, giggling to each other.

"Your grandsons are fine boys," said Dottie.

"Do they play golf?" said Bob. "Maybe they'd like to give Tony a few rounds."

"Take his mind off other things, eh?" said a new voice. Dottie and Bob turned to see Mr. Boggins, Tony's teacher, grinning and weaving a little. "Like his obsession with vampires?"

"What?" said Lord McAshton, instantly alert. "What's that you say?

"Vampires!" said Mr. Boggins.

"It's just a few bad dreams," said Bob, annoyed.

"They're not just dreams, Mr. Thompson," said Mr. Boggins, raising a finger for emphasis. "Tony's troubled. Oh, thank you," he said, as a passing waiter refilled his glass. "He's delusional and has chronic nightmares."

"That's normal for a boy his age," said Dottie.

"With all due respect," said the teacher, "I'm the one with the degrees hanging on the wall."

"With all due respect, you'll be hanging with them in a minute," whispered Dottie angrily.

"He's disturbed!" Mr. Boggins insisted.

McAshton took Bob to one side. "Look here, Thompson, we want no talk of vampires," he said a little uneasily, his eyes swiveling like a startled turkey's to see if any of his important investor guests were listening.

"But, Lord McAshton, it's only—"

"Only, shmoanly, as I believe you say in the U.S.A. People will think we're superstitious, backward, and provincial."

"It's not a serious problem, sir," Bob said, firmly.

"Sounds to me like the lad's head is in the clouds," said Lord McAshton, waving a hand dismissively. "Airy-fairy stuff. Keep a lid on his wilder fancies, there's a good chap."

At that moment the little vampire was standing looking down at Tony, who lay on his back with his eyes tightly closed, feeling that everything was not exactly as it should be.

"Am I all right?" Tony asked. "I didn't get run over?"

"You're all right," said the little vampire. His voice now rang out strong and clear, completely different from the weak, breathy voice before he drank from the cow. However, he did sound a little anxious. "You can look now."

Tony didn't really want to move or do anything. He was sure, despite what the vampire said, that he would find out he was lying mangled on the road after being hit by Rookery's truck. His stomach seemed to be in his shoes, for instance, and he really didn't want to see what that looked like.

But as he felt no pain, he cautiously opened his eyes and took a peek at the world around him. There was no sign of the truck. No sign of the barn and the road, either, and no marks on his body. He patted his stomach and chest and head just to make sure. He was safe and well and in one piece. He even had his glasses on!

Above him a million stars sparkled in the sky, and the brilliant moon shone down like a big friendly face. The comet from his dream was there, too, just visible as a long silvery streak in the night.

"Wow!" said Tony, sitting up.

"It's a magnificent view, isn't it?" said the little vampire, who was staring wistfully at the comet.

"Sure is, dude," said Tony.

"Dude?" said the little vampire. "My name is Rudolph. What's your name?"

"Tony." Tony cleared his throat. "Umm . . . thanks, Rudolph. I guess you saved my life. If you hadn't— Well, I think that truck was going to splat me!"

"If it comes to that," said Rudolph, "I feel guilty. Remember, you wouldn't have been there at all if you hadn't helped me visit the cows. But by doing that, you also saved my—" Rudolph stopped and smiled sadly. "Let's just say you saved *me*. Without your help, I would now be getting weaker and weaker and weaker." He shuddered. "Rookery would probably have caught me! So my thanks are due to you."

There was an awkward silence as Tony digested this. Wow! He guessed he had done Rudolph a big favor after all. So they were friends, in a way. "Shake," he said.

41

"What?"

"Let's shake hands." Tony stuck his hand out, and after a moment Rudolph took it and they shook hands solemnly. Rudolph's hand felt curiously dry and dusty, like old paper.

Tony lay back, looking straight up at the stars, a feeling of contentment stealing over him. Except for one thing. "Say, Rudolph. You're a real vampire, right?"

"Yes," Rudolph said cautiously.

"I didn't know vampires drank cow blood. I thought it had to be human blood, like mine."

Rudolph was silent at this.

Tony wondered if he had said the right thing. He knew it was bad manners to make fun of other people's eating habits. "Hey, sorry if I offended you."

"No, that's fine," said Rudolph. "We have to make do with cow blood. Look, we believe it's not right to bite humans."

"Not right? But it's natural, isn't it?" said Tony. "That's what vampires are for."

"It's not the old days anymore. Normal humans don't accept it like they used to. If people start showing up with bite marks on their necks, it causes all sorts of trouble. So we try to keep a low profile." He sat down. "We've been hunted almost to extinction as it is," he said bitterly.

Tony sat up again, concern written on his face. "I'm sorry," he said. "I didn't mean to pry—"

He stopped suddenly and prodded at the ground. He had just noticed that it was wobbly and felt strangely rubbery under his fingers. He took another look around. The land curved away, as though they were on a little hill, but there was nothing between them and the distant horizon. No trees or buildings blocked the view.

"Where are we, anyway?" Tony said.

"I'm not sure what you call them," said Rudolph. "It's a big thing full of air."

"It's like a trampoline." Tony did an experimental sit-down bounce. "Is it a bouncy castle?" he said.

He stood up and tried a few more bounces, springing around a bemused Rudolph like a kangaroo.

"I don't think it can be any kind of a castle," said Rudolph doubtfully. "There are no fortifications, and anyway the very first arrow would burst it."

"We have these things in play parks and stuff," Tony said authoritatively as he tried higher and higher bounces. "Kids like to bounce on them."

"Really?" said Rudolph, even more doubtful. "It seems incredibly dangerous for a human child."

"It's not dangerous," Tony snorted. "Though there's usually walls to stop you falling off. Maybe this is something else."

"Well, what do you call something big and blown up but shaped more like a ball?"

"I give up. What is it?"

"I don't know! It's not a riddle!" said Rudolph. "I'm asking you a question!"

"Well, I guess a—a balloon? Or a blimp, even." Tony thought about it. "My dad's just made a cool blimp."

"Does it float high above Lord McAshton's manor?"

"Yes."

"I think this must be it, then."

"Waaaah!" wailed Tony, because just then he saw exactly where he was. He clutched at Rudolph for dear life.

Far below he could see the bright lights of McAshton Manor shining out over the landscape. He could even hear music and the chatting of partygoers.

Oh, no, he groaned, my mom and dad are down there! He could hardly believe his eyes, but there was no escaping it. He was high above the tall trees, precariously balanced on top of his father's advertising blimp. McAshton Golf Club and Convention Centre, it proclaimed to the world; he could just see the very tops of the letters from where he was. Perhaps even now his dad was proudly pointing it out to some of the other guests, never imagining his own son was on top of it.

"How did we get up here?" Tony wailed.

"We flew," said Rudolph. "That's one of the things that vampires do."

"And how do we get back down?"

"We'll fly down."

"But I can't fly!"

"If I'm holding on to you, you can fly," said Rudolph. "That's the only rule. Trust me."

"Yeah? But I saw you flying before," said Tony in desperation. "From my window to the ground!"

"That was different."

"Why?"

"That was before I had a cow, remember? I'm all right now."

Tony was not convinced.

"I got you up here, didn't I?" said Rudolph. "How do you think I did that?"

"Well . . ." Tony said doubtfully. "I guess you flew."

"Correct. No mighty stairways here. Now take my hands."

Rudolph held out his hands. Cautiously, as if expecting an electric shock, Tony grasped them.

"First we will just take it gently," said Rudolph, and as he spoke, before Tony was even aware of it, they rose into the air and floated just a few inches above the blimp's surface.

"See?" said Rudolph. "Not too bad, is it?"

Goggle-eyed, Tony stared down at his feet, dangling in nothingness above the blimp.

"Better not look down too much at first," said Rudolph.

"But . . . but I'm floating!"

Gently Rudolph let go of one of Tony's hands.

Tony gritted his teeth and closed his eyes and wobbled just a little, but he stayed in the air.

"Ready?"

Tony, unable to trust himself to speak, forced himself to open his eyes, and nodded.

Moving ever so slowly, Rudolph eased them both out and away from the top of the blimp. Tony felt more and more exposed as its huge soft bulk slipped away from underneath him, like a big whale moving under a sailboat. Hold that thought—pretend we're floating on water. We can't sink.

He felt a little seasick.

There was no protection now from a long fall; it looked like hundreds and hundreds of feet to the ground.

Tony couldn't help wondering what would happen if he fell. Would he splatter, like a watermelon he'd once dropped out of his window in San Diego? Or would he make a deep crater in the ground, like an asteroid smashing into the moon?

What am I doing here? he thought. If I get away with this I'm going to stay at home for the rest of my life and be nice to Mom. And even Dad.

Tony fought to keep his eyes open. He wasn't falling yet. He wasn't falling yet.

Concentrate! Concentrate! Grip tight!

"Relax!" said Rudolph. "As long as I hold you, you're fine. Now we're going to get into proper flying position. That will make it easier."

"I get it!" said Tony. "Like streamlining!"

Rudolph rotated them slowly so they were aiming headfirst. Tony's stomach lurched, and he groaned. Knowing what something is for doesn't always make it easier.

"Are you still all right?" asked Rudolph.

"Yes," Tony managed to gasp. "Let's do it!"

"Then let's go!"

And they were off.

With a sensation that felt as crazy as jumping off a roller coaster, Rudolph and Tony dropped down the side of the blimp. Tony's heart was in his mouth, and the wind streamed his hair back as they picked up speed. They swooped down like eagles before pulling up in a long arc low over a wide open meadow and up again over the roof of McAshton Manor. Its chimneys and turrets and cupolas sped past and fell away behind them. Lights from the party blazed out. It was like flying over the *Titanic* in the middle of the ocean.

"Wow!" yelled Tony in joyful excitement. "That was great!"

The two boys flew off together toward the west, and had soon dwindled to specks in the night sky and were lost among the stars.

Chapter 9

Tony was not completely forgotten by everyone who was charged with his well-being. At the exact moment the boys zoomed above the party at McAshton Manor, Bob's cell phone rang. The sound was loud and piercing, and it came right in the middle of a quiet musical selection that Lord McAshton had requested from the string quartet, as it meant so much to him personally. One of the violinists twanged a string, her concentration disrupted.

"Bob!" said Dottie, horrified. She noticed some of the snootier guests looking down their noses at this basic social error, as if to say, Couldn't you do any better than that, you morons?

"Sorry," he said, blushing with embarrassment as he fumbled to find the phone. "Bob Thompson here," he whispered.

"Mr. Thompson, this is Lorna," said the baby-sitter.

"Lorna!" said Bob, annoyed. "This better be an emergency!"

"Oh, it is! It is, Mr. Thompson! Tony's gone missing!"

"Well, thank heavens for that at least!"

"What is it?" said Dottie.

"Tony's missing."

"*What!*" said Dottie loudly. "Give me that!" and she grabbed the phone from him. "What's going on, Lorna?"

"I've checked and I've checked and I've checked again, but his bed's empty and the window's open and his little red wagon—you know, the one with the green handle that he left on the lawn—that's gone, too!"

"Lorna, calm down!"

"Och, and he looked so sweet in his little vampire costume."

"Did he," Dottie said grimly. "You're sure he's not in the house?"

"Yes! I've looked everywhere. Everywhere! Every—"

"We'll be right there," interrupted Dottie, shutting off the phone and handing it back to Bob. "We have to go."

"Trouble?" asked Lord McAshton, raising an eyebrow.

"Tony's gone missing, sir," Bob said, as he ushered Dottie toward the door.

"Really," McAshton said suspiciously. "Does he often sneak out like this, in the middle of the night?"

"No," Dottie said firmly, "he does not."

"That's good. Oh, one other thing, Thompson," McAshton called loudly after them. "In future, you might try setting your phone to Vibrate."

"I'll set you to vibrate in a minute," muttered Dottie as they left.

Tony was unaware of all this. In fact, he was loving his flight.

It was the most exciting thing he had ever done. He shrieked and screamed as he and Rudolph wheeled and soared and swung and stalled and spun and dropped and banked and carved wide turns in the silvery moonlight, high above the damp, dark fields.

Flying now seemed perfectly natural, the right way for people to travel. The wind in your face, the clouds below, and only the stars above. If birds could do it, and bats and flying squirrels, then why not humans? Flying seemed like the easiest thing in the world, once you got started. Sure, that first big step was a lulu, but once you got over that, everything was fine.

Tony felt he didn't really need to hang on to Rudolph. You just imagined going somewhere, and there you flew. The secret was right there, in front of him, at the tips of his fingers. It was a matter of confidence. You just had to grab it.

As they passed over the cliffs and flew out over the black and turbulent sea, Tony pulled his hand out of Rudolph's, just to try it solo for once.

Suddenly, immediately, he was tumbling straight down out of the sky, head over heels and out of control, with all the flying ability of a lump of concrete!

"Rudolph!" he yelled in fear as he dropped. No more soaring, no more dancing around the fluffy clouds, he was plummeting straight toward some sharp rocks boiling white in the choppy sea.

But with a swooping rush of air, Rudolph dived after him and grabbed his hand. Instantly everything was calm again, and they were flying straight and level.

"Are you all right?" Rudolph asked as they pulled out of the dive and streaked above the cliffs.

Tony was wide-eyed as he gulped for breath. "Yes! Yes!" he gasped. "Okay, Rudolph, I learned my lesson. I won't ever do that again!"

"I hope so," said Rudolph. "Don't jump out of any trees or off any buildings by yourself either. It just won't work. Believe me!"

"I guess not," Tony said wistfully as he watched roads and hedges and trees swish past below. He and Rudolph passed over some houses, their lights glowing a comfortable yellow. Inside people were going about their normal human lives, watching TV or eating dinner, perhaps, unaware that Tony was flying right above them.

"This is so cool! It's great to be a vampire!"

Rudolph snorted. "Membership has its privileges," he said.

"Better than driving!" Tony said as he saw some car headlights moving down a distant lane. "We can just go wherever we want. We don't have to follow the road."

"Well, that's true," said Rudolph. "But on the other hand—"

"Oh, no!" said Tony. He had just seen that the car headlights belonged to a Land Rover.

"What?"

"That car!"

The car turned a corner. Tony peered into the distance. Was that his house over there, with all the lights burning? "I think it's my mom and dad!

"Don't worry, they can't see you up here," Rudolph assured him.

"But—" said Tony.

"No one expects a child to be flying about in the air. Even if they look straight at you, they just rub their eyes. They'd prefer to think they've gone mad rather than believe what they see . . ."

"But—"

"In fact, centuries ago I used to love flying around people at night, flapping my arms and going 'Bullallallallalla!' and frightening their horses. Very immature, I know."

"But they're going home!" Tony managed to say desperately. "My dad will kill me if I'm not home!"

"Will he really?" said Rudolph, amazed and alarmed.

Chapter 10

The Thompsons' Land Rover sped up the driveway. Bob and Dottie could see Lorna standing nervously in the light from the open front door, wringing her hands and looking extremely anxious.

"He really must be missing," Dottie said, getting more agitated herself.

"What is going on with that kid?" said Bob. "He didn't pull these kinds of stunts back home."

"Well, maybe that's the point. This is Scotland, not home. He's eight years old, for heaven's sake."

"Maybe it's jet lag," said Bob as they got out of the car. "He's just not used to flying."

"Oh, Mr. Thompson, Mrs. Thompson," said Lorna. "I checked and checked—"

"Let's see if he took anything with him." said Dottie, pushing past her. "Clothes and so on. Food."

"Passport," said Bob. "Tickets. Money."

They pounded up the stairs, two at a time, Lorna following, helplessly flustered.

Dottie got to Tony's room first, and they rushed in—to find Tony fast asleep in his bed as usual!

"How do you explain this?" Bob asked Lorna, who stared wide-eyed at Tony.

"I know what I saw, and I know what I didn't see," Lorna said defiantly, "and I didn't see him!"

Tony stirred.

"Sshh, you'll wake him," said Dottie.

"Well, he's here, that's the main thing," Bob whispered loudly. He noticed that Tony's window was swinging open, and he crossed the room to close it. As he did so, he passed right under Rudolph, who was clinging to the ceiling, trying hard to make himself look like a lampshade.

Dottie bent over Tony and kissed him gently on his forehead.

Tony tried not to breathe or smile or react in any way, hoping they would all just go away soon. Otherwise how could he explain a strange kid hanging from the ceiling?

Perhaps he would just pretend Rudolph was invisible. If Rudolph was right, the adults would think they were going crazy instead of believing what they saw. A kid couldn't hang from the ceiling. Therefore, he wasn't.

Dottie sniffed the air. "Bob?" she said.

"Do you smell it, too?" said Bob.

"Musty, damp, rotting—" said Dottie.

"Like mushrooms. Or wet dead leaves."

Uh-oh, thought Tony.

"And a hint of cork?" said Lorna.

"Like something's decaying. Dry rot, maybe," said Dottie. "Perhaps Tony's right, and there's something wrong with this place."

Tony could hear the door closing.

"We should get it looked at." Her voice sounded muffled.

"Aw, hon," Bob said, as their voices faded down the stairs. "We had all the surveys and everything. There's nothing wrong with the house."

Tony opened one eye carefully.

"Rudolph!" he whispered fiercely, sure that everyone had gone and not even Lorna remained. "It's safe now!"

Rudolph got down from the ceiling quietly, a little embarrassed. "Um, sorry about the smell," he said. "I haven't taken a bath since 1528."

"Cool! Wait a minute," said Tony, doing some rapid calculations. "Does that mean you're, like, a thousand years old or something?"

"No, I'm nine," said Rudolph.

"Oh," said Tony.

"It's just I've been nine for nearly five centuries." He smiled sadly. "I hardly think I look a thousand, do I? I haven't been able to check a mirror for some time."

"Be my guest," said Tony, pointing to his floor-length mirror. He realized his mistake immediately. "Oh . . . vampires don't reflect, right?"

"No."

"Must be so great being a vampire," said Tony.

"Flying, you mean, and living forever?"

"Yeah! And scaring people! And not having to wash every day or brush your hair!"

"Yes, but . . ." Rudolph sighed. "Some vampires agree with you. They accept our status, even revel in it. They enjoy the taste of human blood, and love living in gloomy big houses in Romania, terrifying the local peasants."

"You don't?"

"No. My brother does, though. He's a traditionalist. But my father insists we seek the way back—"

"Whoa," said Tony. "You've got a family? A mother, too?"

"And a sister. Of course I have a family!"

"I didn't know vampires had families!"

Rudolph gazed out of the window, as if hoping his family would fly past. "I hope they're all safe, with Rookery on the prowl. We were supposed to meet tonight."

"They're coming here?" Tony asked anxiously.

"No need to worry. It's lucky I'm already dead.

Otherwise, maybe my father would think of killing me, too, if he found me talking to a mortal like this."

"Wow," said Tony. "Dads sure are tough. But tonight was fun, huh?"

"Fun?" Rudolph was surprised, but he considered this. "Yes. Yes, it was. You're right! Do you know, I haven't had a friend my own age since I *was* my own age." He stood up, smiling, and made a formal bow. "But I had better go now. I've said too much and led you into great danger."

"You can stay if you want," said Tony casually, secretly hoping Rudolph would say yes. "I mean, with that hunter guy running around out there, maybe you're safer here."

"But—"

"And don't worry about the smell," Tony said, hurriedly. "It doesn't bother me."

"Thank you."

"Only . . . I don't have a coffin for you to sleep in, of course."

"That's fine. Any area where sunlight cannot penetrate will do," said Rudolph. "We call them manchesters."

"Will this do?" Tony asked as he opened his traveling trunk. "Once I've taken all the junk out of it?"

"It will be excellent."

Rudolph's eyes glittered as he looked at the array of expensive toys, robots, computer games, and puzzles that Tony started lifting out. "This is not junk," he said. "It's a treasure trove. What is it all for?"

"I'll show you. Look at this one," Tony said, powering up a pocket computer game. "Here demon monsters from hell threaten a big city, and you have to hunt them down and zap them . . . Umm . . ."

He stopped, embarrassed. Maybe Rudolph would think this was a bit close to home.

"We'll talk about that tomorrow," he said firmly. "My mom would kill me if I stayed up all night."

"I understand. It's a dangerous world we both exist in," Rudolph said gravely as he climbed into the empty trunk. "But as for tomorrow . . . well, we'll see." He settled in and made himself comfortable.

"Is that okay?" said Tony.

"Perfect. Until tonight, then."

"Good night."

Tony closed the lid on Rudolph and leaped into his bed and pulled the covers over himself.

He lay there a minute, thinking over the amazing events of the packed evening.

He had been flying!

He had soared above the clouds!

He had bounced on a blimp!

He had sneaked out of his home, and back, in the middle of the night, and gotten away with it!

He had nearly been run over by a vampire hunter!

He had been in a cow barn! Okay, so that wasn't so great.

But he had made a new friend!

If only Nigel and Flint and the other kids from school could have seen him. What would they say now?

At that thought, Tony's heart sank.

School tomorrow. If he was a vampire, he would never have to go to school again and face those bullies.

"Rudolph, I wanna become a vampire, too," he said suddenly.

"Tony, don't you know what that means?" said Rudolph. His voice was muffled by the trunk, but he sounded horrified.

"Yeah! Doing the most awesome stuff I've ever done in my life!"

Rudolph opened the lid and popped his head out, a warning in his eyes. "No blue skies, Tony. No birds singing. No flowers in the sunlight." He sighed. "That's what I envy you most and what I want more than anything—to walk again in sunshine and feel the warmth of day. Instead I am condemned to the cold stars of everlasting night."

Tony considered this for a moment. "Cool!" he said dreamily, and dozed off.

Chapter 11

Almost instantly, it seemed to Tony, it was morning, and the curtains were torn back and warm sunlight rushed in. The sky was a bright blue, and the birds were singing and twittering in the trees.

Dottie put a vase of fresh flowers on the windowsill. It was just the sort of day Rudolph longed to see.

Tony, on the other hand, turned over and buried his face deep in the pillow, his eyes screwed up tight. He felt he could do with a bit more sleep.

"Any nightmares last night?" Dottie asked.

Tony remembered it all, every bit. "Mom, last night I went flying!"

"That's a nice dream, hon," she said as she collected his scattered socks and popped them into his laundry basket.

"I wasn't dreaming! It was real as you are! I even flew over the party at McAshton Manor!"

"Get ready for breakfast, hon," Dottie said, and rushed out.

Tony thought for a second. Was that a hint of a tear he'd seen in his mother's eye? Was she biting her bottom lip as she did when she didn't want to cry at some soap opera?

Still, as Rudolph said, mortals just didn't believe the evidence of their eyes and ears.

Maybe it really had been a dream. There was one way to find out.

Tony got out of bed and sneaked open the lid of the trunk. A sharp *hissss!* and a rapid *slam!* as someone inside pulled the lid shut told him all he needed to know.

"I wasn't dreaming!" he said to himself.

"Tony! Breakfast!" his mother shouted from the kitchen.

"Coming!" Tony shouted. "Mom! I could eat a cow!"

At that very moment, Farmer McLaughlin was counting his cows in the field near Tony's house. It was a small herd, only five strong, but this morning, no matter how hard he tried, McLaughlin could only get to four.

Where, he wondered, was the fifth beast, Mitsy?

Puzzled, he turned and walked across the road to his barn.

Sunlight streamed in when he threw open the doors. Mitsy hissed loudly and shied back as though scorched. She went as far into the shade at the back of the barn as she could and stood there, looking away.

"Mitsy?" said McLaughlin, scratching his head. "Not feeling too well today, eh? We'll see how you are tomorrow, then."

As the door closed again behind the departing farmer and cool darkness returned to the inside of the barn, Mitsy looked around.

Her eyes gleamed a deep, deep red.

Despite his fears before going to sleep, Tony was bubbling and full of confidence as he jumped out of his mom's car and headed into school that morning.

It was a bright new day. No one else had flown over the village, as he had. No one else had defied a vampire hunter. No one else had made a friend of a genuine, honest-to-goodness real dead vampire!

Nigel and Flint lounged threateningly at the school entrance, blocking his way in.

"Good morning, Vampy," said Nigel.

"Y'mean Wimpy, don't you?" said Flint, sniggering.

"Do you va-a-aant to suck my blo-oo-od?" said Nigel, exposing his neck.

"Well, you can't," said Flint, holding up a little homemade cross. "We've got defenses!"

"Outta my way, losers," Tony said defiantly. "I've got things to do. And of course I've gotta be home by sundown. I'm planning a busy night."

He pushed his way between Nigel and Flint. They were so astonished by Tony's action that they fell over on their rear ends.

They looked at each other, mouths gaping open, as Tony strode purposefully past them and into school.

Some of the other kids, who had been hanging around, as usual, waiting for the fight of the day, started tittering.

"Watch it," Nigel warned them menacingly. They shut up instantly.

"Let's get the little creep," said Flint.

They jumped up and chased after Tony. Nigel pulled a string of garlic bulbs from his pocket.

"Take this, bat-boy!" he said.

Tony turned and got clobbered on the head. While he was dazed, Flint wrestled him to the floor.

The expected fight was under way. The other kids gathered around, cheering and chanting.

This time Tony fought back.

Chapter 12

"I'm disappointed in you, Tony," said Dottie, dabbing his nose with a tissue a little bit later. "Fighting the McAshton boys, of all people! Your father will be mad when he hears." She sighed. "It embarrasses him with Lord McAshton. Makes his life harder."

Tony had not expected his mother to understand. He just wished she did not have to do the first aid in his bedroom, with Rudolph still in the trunk a few inches from her.

"Sorry, Mom," he said. "But they started it!"

She looked down at him. A thin trail of blood dribbled from one of his nostrils. She started making a couple of small wads of tissue.

In the darkness of the trunk, Rudolph's eyes snapped open.

Blood.

Human blood.

And, oh, so close! His fangs started to lengthen, his eyes glowed a deep red, like Mitsy's.

"Last night your teacher told me all about you," said Dottie.

"What about me?"

"That you talk about vampires in class. No wonder your friends make fun of you."

"They're not my friends!"

"And you'll never make any friends if you carry on like this. The McAshton boys are the loveliest, most popular boys in school. Why can't you try to get on with them?"

"They're bullies!" Tony said crossly. "No one really likes them. The other kids are just scared of them!"

"Really, Tony! Don't be silly. Now, hold still." She plugged his nose with the wads of tissue, which stuck out like walrus tusks. "There you go. You look great." She smiled.

Just then Tony heard the softest of noises from the trunk. Rudolph must be awake! And at the same moment Dottie sniffed the air.

"There it is again," she said. "That strange smell."

"I do have a friend, but he's not here right now," Tony said quickly and very loudly, hoping Rudolph would get the message.

"Really?" Dottie said, distracted. "At school?"

"Well, no."

"So he's not at school? But he's your age, isn't he?"

"Hard to say. I guess."

Dottie's eyes narrowed in suspicion.

Tony realized the conversation was heading into an awkward area. "His parents, er, travel a lot. They teach him as they go."

"What's he like?"

"Cool!"

"Well, I'm sure we'd like to meet him. Why don't you invite him for a sleepover?"

"I already did," Tony said, giggling.

"Good! That's a start." She ruffled his hair and stood up. Tony listened as hard as he could. Rudolph was silent. He must have gone to sleep again.

Trouble over.

"What are these toys and things doing out?"

Uh-oh. Spoke too soon.

Dottie picked up one of the robots from the floor and moved toward the trunk.

Tony groaned, thinking fast. "Mom!" he said. "I'm using them for a school project. Please put him back."

Dottie hesitated, then set the robot down on top of the trunk. "Okay, but make sure you put them away when you're finished. First, you'd better get some rest."

"But, Mom, I feel fine."

"Rest!" she said, closing the door behind her.

Dottie turned to find her unsmiling husband in the corridor, clasping a golf club like a baseball bat and looking as though he meant business.

"What are you going to do with that?" she said, shocked.

"I did think of hitting him into the middle of next week with it," said Bob. "But no. No, it's time I taught Tony how to be a man. We're going to play golf."

It was cold and breezy on the seaside golf course Bob had picked for this first lesson, very different from the morning. Tony was learning that weather could be changeable in Scotland, even in just one day. Wind-whipped waves smashed against the coastal rocks, sending spray high into the air and dampening his face. Seagulls danced and dive-bombed in the air currents, as free as—well, as free as birds. Or vampires!

Tony shivered, trying hard not to look at the seagulls. If he did, his mind would wander to memories of his own experience of flying and soaring through the piled-up clouds. He tried instead to keep focused on what his dad was saying as he worked through the basic rules of the game of golf.

The brisk breeze snapped at the flag as they walked onto a green.

"A lot of self-discipline is needed in golf, Tony," Bob said as he pulled his putter out of his big tartan-patterned golf bag. "Courtesy and manners, too, and gentlemanly behavior. And you have to keep your own score."

He tapped his ball toward the hole. It stopped about three feet short.

"Nuts!" he said. "Still, you'll give me that one, eh?"

"Sure, Dad," said Tony. "I guess."

Bob scooped up his ball and pocketed it. Tony tapped his own ball. It rolled to within six inches of the hole.

"Better just knock it in," said Bob, "since you're so close."

"Okay." But Tony miscalculated, and the ball bobbled around the hole without dropping in.

"Bad luck! Try again."

This time Tony sank the putt.

"Well done, but I think I win that one," Bob said as he filled in his card.

Tony cast a fearful eye toward the sun, which was only occasionally visible, a silvery disk peeking through the scudding black clouds. He couldn't help noticing that curtains of rain seemed to be heading straight toward them from over the gun-metal gray sea, where white caps were dancing on the waves.

"Dad, what time does the sun go down?"

"Don't worry, not for a long time yet."

"But when? I have to be home before it sets."

"What's the big hurry? We've still got seventeen holes to play."

Tony groaned at this news.

"What's the matter? Not tired, are you?" said Bob. "I thought you wanted to learn golf?"

"I'd rather learn to fly."

"Tony!" Bob said angrily. "You've got to stop it with these crazy ideas!" He took a few deep breaths and calmed down. "Maybe when you're a little older, eh?" He clapped his son on the back, manfully.

"Do you really think I'm crazy, Dad?" said Tony.

"Umm . . . no. But, son, listen to me. Vampires belong in superstitions and old horror movies. Not in your bedroom, and not now."

"How'd you know a vampire's there now?" said Tony, alarmed.

Bob frowned, and Tony realized he'd nearly given Rudolph away. "Sorry, Dad," he said. "Not funny, right?"

"Not very." Bob sighed. "Look, son, I know I've been rough on you lately, and I blame myself partly. I've been very busy, and I haven't been paying enough attention to you. That's one reason we're here this afternoon. But look at it from my point of view. Your teachers and Lord McAshton are breathing down my neck. Well, I'm sorry, Tony, that's an extra pressure I don't need. All this fighting and talk of vampires and frightening kids at school has got to stop."

"Gee, Dad, I'm sorry. But—"

"You're making me a laughingstock!"

"But—"

"But nothing! You know there are no such things as vampires!"

"Oh, I guess," said Tony, giving in finally.

He made a vow with himself. He'd show them, prove everybody wrong! But for now he put on a brave face and looked his dad straight in the eye. "Let's play golf!" he announced.

"That's my boy!" said Bob, beaming. He picked up his golf bag and started running away. "Come on, Tiger," he called over his shoulder. "Race you to the next tee!"

"Aww, Dad, that's not fair!"

Hours later, after the sun had set, Bob crunched his Land Rover to a halt outside the house.

"Home sweet home," he said, but Tony was already out of the car and running inside.

He pounded up the stairs two at a time, as fast as his legs could carry him, hoping that he was not too late.

He burst into his bedroom—

To find the trunk open and empty. Rudolph had gotten up and left.

"Rudolph!" he wailed.

But there was no answer. The window was

slightly open, and the curtains billowed in the draft. Tony's vampire drawings were being blown all over the floor.

He slowly picked them all up, except the one of the gold amulet, which he couldn't find, and put them back on his desk, his eyes full of tears.

He sat down and stared out of the window, feeling like the loneliest boy in the world.

Chapter 13

Tony did not feel like eating dinner that evening. He pushed his food around the plate, kicking his legs and feeling miserable as his dad chattered on about their day.

"And then I was ten up with eight to play," said Bob. "Never had such a lead before!"

"And that's when you stopped and came home?" Dottie asked.

"No! I pressed home my advantage, as Lord McAshton would say."

"I think you should have come home earlier."

"Garbage! We were having a great time! The exercise did Tony good!"

Dottie glanced at Tony and smiled encouragingly. "Did you have a great time, hon?"

Tony tried to look happy but failed. "Mom, I don't feel so good. May I be excused?"

"Not until you've finished what's on your plate," said Bob. "You're a growing boy. You need to eat, build up those muscles!"

"But—"

"Besides, we've still got to describe the rest of the back nine to your mom."

"You run along, hon," said Dottie. "Bob, he's got a chill. You shouldn't have kept him out so long."

"Thanks, Mom," said Tony morosely, sliding out of his chair and walking slowly out of the room, his head bowed. "Good night."

"Good night, hon," said Dottie.

Perhaps it had been some sort of fevered dream after all, Tony thought as he climbed into bed. He lay there for a while, staring at the ceiling, wondering how you could tell what was a dream and what was real. He had heard that people tried pinching themselves to see if they were awake, but he had also heard that you could pinch yourself in a dream. If that was so, what was the use?

After a short while his thoughts drifted to another interesting topic: why was the ceiling flickering? Ripples and reflections from puddles of water seemed to be dancing above his head.

Weird. He lay there, enjoying the effect.

And, he noticed, the room seemed to be getting cooler. A strange drip, drip, drip of water was coming from somewhere, but it didn't sound like a bathroom faucet.

There was a breath of wind, too, a salty sea breeze, but softer and warmer than the one at the golf course. And the gentle sound of waves lapping on a beach. And the thunder of a horse's hooves in the hard sand.

Tony sat up.

He seemed to be sitting in his bed, all right, but it was just inside a cave overlooking the ocean. Outside, the day—and it was day, midmorning perhaps—was bright and sunny.

Tony could see an ancient ship wrecked on the rocks offshore. Its wooden hull was knocked through with holes. Tattered sails hung limp from three tall masts, one of which was broken near the top. It looked like a pirate ship from one of his books.

And there was the horse he had heard, a big white one, just pulling up, snorting and stamping its feet and tossing its head.

A glamorous young redheaded woman rode it, sidesaddle. She was dressed almost like a queen, in heavy old-fashioned clothes. A huge red velvet cloak protected her richly embroidered dress.

The woman gazed out at the wreck, then glanced down at the sand, and then looked directly at Tony. He shrank back as she climbed down off the horse and started walking into the cave toward him, her big eyes fixing him to the spot.

Tony knew he could not run away. Who was she and what did she want? The woman lifted the hem of her heavy cape as she came deeper into the cave, taking care not to step in the puddles.

She went straight past Tony as though he was invisible and dropped to her knees. Only then did he notice that someone else was in the cave with them: a young man, pale and elegant and sick-looking, lying on the ground by the end of Tony's bed. He looked dashing and romantic, with flowing dark hair.

With a gasp, Tony recognized him. It was Von, the young vampire from his dream, the one who had dived off the cliff after the jewel. Now he lay pale and unconscious right by Tony's bed. Something gold and gleaming was clenched in Von's right hand.

The woman unclasped the large, ornate brooch that held her cloak fastened, a brooch with a coat of arms. Tony could see it clearly: a pair of deer with huge antlers and, above them, two crossed swords.

She spread the cloak over Von's body, and then, clearly fascinated, she reached for his hand and prised open his stiff, clammy fingers, revealing the red jewel itself—the stone!

She held it up, admiring the way the stone absorbed and reflected the glittering shards of sunlight from the sparkling waves outside.

Wham! A man's hand grabbed her wrist and she screamed.

Von was awake! He hissed and bared his fangs!

Tony jumped back, shocked, and clunked his head on the wall. *Knock!* it went. *Knock! Knock! Knock!*

Tony jerked awake. He was back in his own bedroom.

Knock! Knock! The sound came from the window.

Tony leaped out of bed and opened it, to see a dark shape standing outside. "Rudolph! You came back!"

"I had to come back," Rudolph said wearily, stepping into the room and looking serious. He was wiping his mouth with the back of his hand. Tony didn't want to ask what he'd been doing, but he guessed Rudolph could now find his own way to Farmer McLaughlin's barn.

"Can we go flying again?" Tony asked eagerly.

"No, it's far too dangerous," Rudolph said grimly. "I had to come back because of this." He held up Tony's drawing of the jeweled amulet with the red stone set in the middle of it—the stone he had just seen. "This is what we're looking for!"

"That?" said Tony, surprised. "Oh, you can have that."

"Where did you get it?"

"Get it? I drew it."

"I mean the real thing, the original object. Where did you see it?"

Tony was reluctant to admit that the amulet was part of his dream for fear that Rudolph wouldn't take him seriously and might disappear again. Tony narrowed his eyes thoughtfully. Maybe they could strike a bargain. "I'll tell you only if you take me flying again."

"Tony," said Rudolph, annoyed, "this isn't a game!"

Tony was crestfallen. Oops.

Rudolph looked out of the window toward the bright moon, and his shoulders sagged as if he was admitting defeat. He turned back to Tony. "It isn't a game. But you win anyway."

"You mean—" said Tony, thrilled.

Before he could say anything else Rudolph had grabbed him by the hand and pulled him out of his bedroom window and up into the sky. Once more they were soaring through billowing clouds carved out of moonlit silver.

Five short minutes later they were descending slowly toward the graveyard of the ruined church. Rudolph, clearly disappointed at something, scoured the area as they came down.

"Not yet," he muttered as they landed. Tony didn't want to interrupt and ask what he meant. Rudolph didn't seem to be in a good mood, and Tony was all too aware that he didn't know enough about vampires and their moods.

Skeptically, Tony surveyed the cracked columns, the ivy-infested walls, and the tall old tombstones.

Not a breath of wind disturbed the leaves. Nothing moved. Maybe it was dangerous to come here with Rudolph. The place looked pretty spooky, and Tony wondered why Rudolph had brought him here. To put him off the realities of vampire life, perhaps.

"The flying part I liked," said Tony eventually, just to break the silence. "I could get used to that! But I'm not so sure about all this." He waved a hand at the ranks of dark and silent graves.

Rudolph wasn't listening to him. He was looking up to the sky. The comet was brighter this night and nearer the moon.

"Okay, I kept my part of the agreement," he said. "Now, where did you see this amulet?"

"Well, uh," said Tony, feeling a little guilty now, as though he had tricked Rudolph, "I haven't seen the real thing, but I have seen it in my dreams."

"You've never seen the real thing anywhere?" said Rudolph, disappointed.

"No. Like I said, I dreamed it all—the amulet, the comet, the moon, the vampires, the hunter. You." There was a pause. Tony looked up at the comet, wishing he could say something more helpful. "Perhaps that means something, my dreaming."

Rudolph snorted.

Tony tried again. "Does this gold amulet mean something to you?"

"Can't say. It's a secret," said Rudolph shortly.

"Oh, c'mon Rudolph!" said Tony. "Who am I gonna tell? Who's gonna believe me?"

Rudolph looked at him with cold, tired eyes. He did look about a thousand years old then.

"If you tell me the secret," said Tony, "maybe it will help somehow."

"How?"

"I don't know."

Rudolph mulled it over for a second and then made a decision. He smiled, and his old warmth was back. Tony exhaled in relief.

"All right," Rudolph said. "Sorry. Very rude of me. You're probably right. Your dream must mean something. But what? Father might know." He pointed up at the sky. "Do you know what that is?"

"A comet. Comet Forsey."

"To you, maybe. We call it the Comet Attamon. It's the comet of the lost souls and a key to ending our curse."

"What curse?"

"The curse of being a vampire." Rudolph sighed. "The appetite for human blood and the inability to walk about in daylight. We've tried many things to cure our fear of the light, to become accepted in the world. One of our mad cousins even went about dressed all in yellow for ten years."

"Did it work?"

"No. Neither did a million other schemes.

Three centuries ago we missed our greatest chance. At the next Gathering in two nights' time we'll miss it again for another three hundred years if we don't have the stone." He pointed at Tony's drawing. "The Stone of Attamon at the center of the amulet is a little piece of the comet, a fragment that fell to earth centuries ago. A great magician embedded it in the amulet and entrusted it to us to use when the time was right. And then we lost it three hundred years ago."

"When I saw it fall into the ocean!"

Rudolph looked at Tony, impressed. "You're right. My uncle Von tried to save it. We've never seen him since, from that night to this, though we've looked. Our wandering has never ended."

Tony put a hand on Rudolph's shoulder. "I'll help you find it. That must be what my dream really means."

"I hope you're right—"

Rudolph fell silent. A spooky wind from nowhere started tossing the crowns of the trees and blowing leaves around in furious circles.

"Hide!" said Rudolph. "My parents are coming!"

Chapter 14

Far above the graves, their capes billowing in the wind, two utterly strange people stood on the ruins of a massive stone wall, gazing out at the distant horizon. They looked like ancient gods surveying their domain—powerful, austere, unfriendly, and overall a bit skinny and bony. Tony needed no second urging from Rudolph. He scampered off to hide behind a tombstone. Fearful, he peered out.

The new arrivals had pale, sad faces and hollow eyes. They seemed to be covered with centuries of dust, but Tony recognized them from his dream.

"Father! Mother!" Rudolph called.

As if they had only just noticed him, they glanced down. Freda, his mother, smiled, and her face was transformed into a look of joy.

"Rudolph!" she said. "At last!"

Frederick and Freda floated down to join him, their capes streaming behind them. Rudolph ran to them, hugging them both tightly.

Freda stroked his head. "Thank the stars you're safe," she said. "We were afraid—"

"That Rookery had staked me?" said Rudolph. "He almost did. He's in the area."

"These are dangerous times," said Frederick, shaking his head. "Where are Gregory and Anna?"

"I haven't seen them," said Rudolph.

"Yoo-hoo!" said a spectral young voice.

Out of nowhere, a little girl popped into existence in a puff of dust, sitting on a short block of broken stone a few feet from Rudolph.

Tony stared. If Mr. Boggins had been there, he would have told him to shut his mouth. The girl was about Tony's age, with long blond hair, and wearing a delicately embroidered red dress overlaid with black lace. She sat there, calmly fanning her face with an elegant little folding fan as though it was the most natural thing in the world to appear just like that.

"I took the road less traveled," she said. "And—"

"And you got lost," Frederick said grimly. He looked around at his family. "There's still one missing."

Tony heard a rumbling in the air and felt the ground vibrating, as though a herd of cattle was stampeding through the next valley.

"That'll be the little beast now," said Freda, smiling.

The rumbling grew louder and louder, and then a patch of ground erupted in mud and stones.

A blurred shape shot up out of the earth and came to a sudden stop, shaking itself free of dirt and revealing the figure of Gregory, Rudolph's punkish teenage brother. He wore a long coat and had multicolored hair.

"I found another really great place for us to stay," he said sarcastically, pointing down the hole.

"Good work!" said Freda, trying to ruffle his hair.

Gregory grimaced and jerked his head away irritably.

"You must never wander so far again," said Frederick. "We're at a critical time—"

"Now that we're all here, did you get any news of the stone?" Rudolph asked excitedly.

"Don't interrupt your father!" Frederick said, angry.

"Because I—"

"Rudolph!"

Frederick looked up at the comet and spread his arms wide. "We're at a critical time, and I must needs bend all my energies to seeking our goal. Rookery is abroad. We must tread still in the shadows and the dark places . . . cling to the night."

This speech was so familiar to Rudolph, Anna, and Gregory that they could join in, and they did.

"And you must all stay together," said Gregory, "For I cannot be searching—"

"For the Stone of Attamon," said Anna, "and searching for you children—"

"At the same time," said Rudolph. "You're causing great worry—"

"To your poor mother and me," said all of them together.

"Now, children . . ." said Freda, as Frederick glowered.

"But, Father!" said Rudolph. "I've—"

"Rudolph! Hold fast, boy! I have one last thing to say."

"Huh! That'll be the night!" said Gregory.

"It's important!" said Rudolph. "I've found a clue!"

"You?" said Frederick disdainfully. "You're but nine years old."

"So you keep reminding me!"

"How could you possibly understand the subtleties of that which we seek?"

Tony felt restless, his heart pounding in his chest. Why didn't Frederick just listen to Rudolph for one minute? Were all fathers the same? You try to tell them something, but they don't listen. They just go on thinking and talking about whatever they want to think and talk about.

Just then Tony noticed that Gregory was looking in his direction, his nose twitching, his ears flicking. He was listening, sniffing the air.

Oh, no! thought Tony. I've been spotted!

Before Tony could duck back behind the tombstone, Gregory's eyes locked on to him, and Gregory smiled a wolfish, fanged smile.

Suddenly there was a whoosh through the air, then a blur—and Gregory was standing right beside him!

"Aha!" said Gregory, his eyes glinting. "What have we here?" As he reached out toward Tony there was another whoosh and Rudolph stood between them.

"No!" said Rudolph. "He's—he's a friend!"

"A friend?" Gregory said evilly. "I don't think so, brother."

"Gregory," said Freda, "what is going on?"

Tony had no choice. He stepped out into the open. Everyone stared at him in surprise. Perhaps his modern outfit looked strange to them.

"I can't remember that we have any friends," said Frederick, scratching his chin.

"Oh, but he does look nice," said Anna, her eyes glinting as she looked Tony up and down. Her fan fluttered a little more quickly. "What clan is he from, Rudy?"

"Yes, Rudy," Gregory said mockingly. "Why don't you tell us? Which clan of the noble undead does this fine vampirelet hail from?"

"He's not from any clan." Rudolph sounded sheepish. "He's Tony. He's a mortal."

"Ooooh!" squeaked Anna, excited at the danger.

"A mortal!" said Frederick, thunderstruck.

"Oh, Rudy," said Freda. "Is this wise?"

"Just as I thought!" said Gregory. "And a tasty-looking sample, too."

Frederick stepped forward and loomed over Tony, whose knees started to shake. Frederick was very tall and very terrifying. His eyes were like pools of pure black that you could fall into forever and ever.

And his fangs . . . they were long and sharp and gleaming, like ivory daggers.

Frederick reached out and placed one bony finger under Tony's chin, lifting him effortlessly into the air. Tony's legs kicked uselessly a few feet above the ground as Frederick inspected his neck.

"I didn't bite him!" said Rudolph. "I wouldn't!"

"I'm Rudolph's f-friend," stammered Tony, with some difficulty. "P-pleased to meet you."

"You could be many things to my son," said Frederick coldly. "Dinner, perhaps. But you could never be his friend. Now, what are we going to do with you?"

Gregory snorted. "You have to ask?"

"Gregory," said Freda, "you know we don't bite humans."

"What kind of vampires are we?" Gregory said, disgusted.

"The kind that do not bite humans."

"Tony likes vampires," said Rudolph. "That's what I've been trying to tell you. He dreams of us."

"Am I in your dreams, mortal?" said Anna, peering over her fan with her big gray eyes.

"And he knows about the Stone of Attamon!" said Rudolph. "In fact—" He stopped, having seen Frederick's face. Already pale, it now went completely white.

"Remember your low blood pressure," said Freda.

"He knows of the stone?" said Frederick, his eyes sparking with anger as he stared down at Tony. "The cunning devil wangled the information out of you, did he? He's a spy! Rookery's little helper!"

"Darling . . ." said Freda.

"Perhaps Gregory is right," said Frederick.

"Yess-s-s!!" shouted Gregory, punching the air. "At last!"

"No!" shouted Rudolph.

"Darling, consider the consequences of your actions." Balancing Tony with her own finger under his chin, Freda took him from her husband. She smiled. "He does not look like a spy, does he?"

" 'Mortal spies in cunning disguise, wearing old school ties and telling lies,' " said Gregory darkly. "That's what we've always been taught, isn't it?"

Freda put Tony down next to Rudolph. Tony

felt that his jaw was about to break. He had never tried dangling by his chin before, and now he knew why.

"He saved me from Rookery," Rudolph said, putting a protective hand on Tony's shoulder.

"Oh, thank you, Tony, that was kind of you," said Freda, smiling gently.

"My very own son, beholden to a mortal for his existence?" said Frederick, shaking his head. "A likely story!"

"Rudolph spent last night in my trunk," said Tony. "In my house!"

Frederick actually laughed. "Even more likely! Imagine!"

"It's the truth, Father," said Rudolph. "We can trust Tony."

"Nonsense!"

Freda touched Frederick's arm. "Even Rudolph couldn't make up such a wild story. Could you, dear?"

Rudolph looked at her with his big eyes and shook his head, as innocent-looking as a small vampire could be.

"Frederick, mortal or not, he is just a boy," Freda whispered in her husband's ear. "But if you insist on eating him, go ahead."

Tony gulped.

"I never said I was going to eat him," Frederick said irritably. "As if we don't have enough to worry about at the moment."

Freda smiled serenely, her job done.

"It's madness, but"—Frederick pointed to the exit from the church grounds—"you may leave us."

"But Rudolph—" said Tony.

"—was wrong to befriend you," said Frederick. "Leave us, I say!"

"But what about—"

"*Leave us!*" Frederick shrieked. He seemed to grow in size, and his eyes blazed furiously.

Terrified, Tony turned and ran away from the vampire family, blinking away tears.

Chapter 15

"Now, Rudolph," said Frederick, "you've made a serious, serious error in judgment, mixing a mortal up in our quest."

"But he sees dream images—"

"Hush, I say! There's no—"

Phut-Woooooshh! Something small zipped past Frederick's ear. "What was that?"

The vampires looked around, taken by surprise.

Tony had heard the strange sound, too, as he ran away. He looked back to see what it was, and he tripped over a long, strange tube snaking across the path and fell headlong to the ground, scraping his hands and knees.

Phut-woooooshh! Ping!

There it was again!

Phut-wooooshh! Klak!

This time Tony caught a glimpse of something like a small dart flying through the air. Then came the strange cries and shrieks, like the sounds in his dreams—the cries of vampires trying to escape from the vampire hunter!

Tony took a chance and raised his head to peek over a low wall. In the distance he could see Freda gathering her children around her. Then she seemed to melt into the undergrowth on the ruined church grounds, like a ghost. Frederick, just as in the dream, stood tall, his skull-like head twisting this way and that as he sought his hidden enemy.

Tony saw him first, crouching behind a tombstone, thirty yards off. It was the first time he had seen him clearly, but it was definitely Rookery, carrying what looked like a high-tech vacuum cleaner, but holding it like a gun. He stood, lifted the weapon, pointed it at Frederick, and pulled the trigger.

Phut-woooosh! Another small wooden stake shot out of the weapon, whizzed past Frederick's head, and pinged into a wall. Frederick raised his cape and hissed like all the snakes in hell.

Rookery stepped closer, smiling grimly, more confident now. Tony could see a tube coming out of the back of the stake gun, the same tube that he had just tripped over. It ran to Rookery's big truck, where a quiet air compressor was chugging away.

Without even stopping to think, Tony whipped out his penknife and cut the tube.

Rookery pulled the trigger again.

Pffft! A wooden stake dribbled out of the end of the gun and dropped uselessly to the ground.

"What the—" said Rookery, startled.

"The age of chivalry is not yet dead!" squealed Anna. She watched excitedly from the shadows until her mother put a hand over her mouth and dragged her away to safety.

Frederick took his opportunity. He sprang up and with a roar of fury swung his arms out and up and, without even connecting, managed to throw Rookery over a low wall.

"Aaaargh!" yelled Rookery. He flew high through the air and plunged into a thicket of brambles, dazed.

Frederick pressed his advantage and leaped after him. Rookery pushed aside his heavy gun and whipped out a new weapon—a large cross.

Frederick scowled and stopped in his tracks.

Rookery hit a switch and the cross flickered with a harsh ultraviolet light. It was electric! Rookery thrust it in Frederick's face.

Frederick shrieked in pain as he was slammed back. He twirled his cape over his head and seemed to shiver and shake and shrink until finally he disappeared. There was a loud rustle in the undergrowth and he was gone.

Rookery lay on the ground, sweating and breathing heavily. He looked very angry.

Tony was suddenly aware that Rudolph and his family had escaped and he was alone in a graveyard in the middle of the night with a large and violent man. No one had the faintest idea where he was and wouldn't know he was missing for hours yet.

Trying not to make any noise, he turned and started to creep away.

Rookery heard him first, then saw him.

"Hoi!" he yelled. "Not you again!"

Tony panicked and ran as fast as he could, jumping over rocks and graves and pushing through bushes and high grass. The paths were slippery with fallen leaves that hid puddles. Tony could hear the lumbering footsteps of Rookery splashing along behind him, getting closer and closer and closer, as in a nightmare.

And worse . . . Tony ran into a dead end! A great impenetrable tangle of brambles and weeds lay in his path.

He skidded to a stop. There was nowhere to go. He turned around. Rookery came up warily, panting, holding his electric cross up in front of him.

Tony backed away, step by step.

The cross had no effect. Rookery, surprised, gave it a whack with the palm of his hand and held it up again. Nothing. He stared at Tony with furrowed eyebrows and maybe even a hint of fear in his eyes.

"What kind of bloodsucker are you, anyway?" he whispered. "This should—"

"There's no such thing as vampires!" Tony yelled. "My dad said so!"

"Oh!" said Rookery, getting it now. "A little bleeding-heart sympathizer, are you? Well, watch where your little heart bleeds 'cause they'll turn on you one day and gobble you up!"

He threw aside his cross and leaped forward, reaching out with his enormous hairy hands.

Tony took one last step back and disappeared from sight down a small hole. Half scrabbling, half falling, he must have dropped thirty or more feet in a rattle of rocks and mud before he landed in complete darkness on a damp stone floor, his heart beating louder than a drum, his nose full of dirt.

Suddenly someone or something put a dry little hand over his mouth and dragged him down a dark tunnel.

Rookery peered down the hole carefully, as if expecting Tony to jump back out like a magical jack-in-the-box. To be on the safe side, he pulled out his homemade flare pistol and fired it down into the darkness underground.

"Take that, you traitor!"

The flare gleamed bright orange, hissing loudly and lighting up Rookery's grinning face with a demonic glow.

"Hey you, Jimmy!" came a voice from behind

him. Rookery turned around to see a small man in a big crash helmet sitting on a tiny motor scooter. It was the cemetery caretaker. "What d'you think you're doing?"

"None of your business, matey," said Rookery.

"It is when you're in my ol' cemetery. Visiting hours are from dawn to dusk." Just then the caretaker noticed the dying glow of the flare. "And what d'you think you're doing letting off fireworks at your age? Now clear out."

Rookery's finger twitched on the trigger of his flare pistol, but then he thought better of blasting the caretaker into a newer cemetery. It might be hard to explain, so he holstered the flare pistol.

"I'm terribly sorry," he said in his most charming voice. "It won't happen again."

"Well, all right," said the caretaker. "See that it doesn't."

With that he started up his whiny little vehicle and weaved off into the mist, back to the rectory. He pootled down the track, across a little wooden bridge, and up the hill to his temporary home. He leaned his scooter against the For Sale sign and went inside.

All the time Rookery watched, scratching his chin thoughtfully.

Chapter 16

"It's all right, Tony," said Rudolph. "It's only us."

Tony opened his eyes. He was lying on his back, with the whole vampire family standing around him. They were in some kind of underground room, probably the old crypt under the church. Huge stone blocks formed the walls. Gloomy tunnels led off in every direction, studded with alcoves full of statues, jars, and bones.

Tony struggled to his feet and brushed off his muddied clothes. He blew his nose on his handkerchief and a couple of clods of mud flew out. Then he could smell the tunnels—damp soil and fungus.

"What you just did was foolish," said Frederick.

"Foolish maybe, but brave, very brave," said Freda.

"Well, thanks," said Tony. He didn't know what else to say.

Anna's eyes shone with admiration, and Rudolph beamed happily, but Gregory looked annoyed. He glowered at Tony.

"Good thing you cut that tube," said Rudolph.

"I saw it in front of me, and I just went for it. I didn't even think— *waaah!*"

Gregory pounced. Swift as a blur he knocked Tony down and sat on his chest, grinning wildly.

"Gregory!" shouted Frederick as he hauled him off. "What's the meaning of this?"

" 'I saw it in front of me, and I just went for it'!" said Gregory, laughing like a maniac. " 'I didn't even think!' "

"Tony may have saved your skin. Doesn't that count for anything with you?"

"A likely story—you said it yourself. Don't be fooled—he's in with Rookery. I bet Tony led him to us in the first place!"

Frederick pointed down one of the corridors. "Go! Leave us and prepare the sleeping room. I will speak to you later."

Gregory slunk off, hands in pockets, shoulders slumped. Muttering to himself, he aimed a kick at a fat black rat that made the mistake of getting in his way.

"I must apologize, Tony," Freda said sweetly. "It's his adolescent desires, poor lambkin. He can't always control them."

Frederick knelt down by Tony. "Let's see if he did any damage," he said.

He was much friendlier than the first time he had inspected Tony. His eyes were deep, yes, but wise with centuries of experience.

As he leaned forward a heavy golden circlet secured on a chain fell out of Frederick's tunic and dangled in front of Tony's eyes. He recognized it immediately. There was a big hole in the middle where the Stone of Attamon should have been! This was it, the remaining half of the magical amulet that Tony kept seeing in his dream!

Mesmerized, he reached out and grabbed it. Frederick pulled back.

"No, Tony. I need that to summon the Gathering of the Clan."

He tried to pry Tony's fingers off the amulet, but Tony would not or could not let go.

Frederick began to get alarmed. "No!" he shouted. "Get off! Get off!"

It was as though Tony's fingers were fused to the circlet. They started glowing golden red, as if they had caught fire.

"No!" Frederick cried again.

Tony's eyes closed, and he fell back into his world of dreams. This time he saw not an unfolding story but a series of quick images, flashbacks to things he had already seen, as if his brain was fast-forwarding a videotape.

In one image the vampires chanted as they raised the amulet. Rookery thundered closer. The stone flipped end over end into the ocean. Von desperately dived into the water after it. Von pressed the Stone of Attamon into Elizabeth's hands. Elizabeth was wearing her cloak, with her coat of arms prominently displayed.

The coat of arms was struck by lightning and burst into flames.

Tony opened his eyes and shivered. He was back in the cave, and Frederick was looking at his empty circlet.

"That has never happened before. I had a vision from our past," Frederick said. He glanced at Tony in amazement. "We shared it, did we not? You saw the same things?"

Tony nodded. "You and the moon and the comet . . ."

"The ceremony. And Von . . ."

"See, I told you that Tony dreams about us!" said Rudolph.

"The boy indeed has sympathy for our kind," said Freda.

"Ooh, lovely," said Anna, her eyes sparkling.

"If this vision is right," Frederick said in wonder, "Von found the stone." He paced around, thinking. "The legends must be true. He escaped from the sea, was shipwrecked on a distant shore . . ."

"But where is Von now?" Freda said wearily.

"That was hundreds of years ago. There are many coastlines in this world. We cannot search them all!"

"He must have come ashore near here. Perhaps that is why we have been drawn here after all these years. Surely the power of the stone is growing as the time nears."

"That does sound promising. But what shall we do now?" Freda asked.

"In my vision there was a mortal woman I've never seen before, bearing a strange coat of arms," said Frederick.

"That brooch? Yes," said Tony. "I saw it clearly."

"That could mean the answer to our most desperate desires. Discover the identity of the family that crest belongs to, and the Stone of Attamon will surely be nearby, among their treasures," said Frederick. "But how?"

"I can help you," Tony said eagerly.

"No!"

"But I can go looking in the daytime . . ."

"Absolutely not!"

". . . when you can't even move."

"Thrice no, sir!" said Frederick. "It's too dangerous to trust a mortal with our affairs. If Rookery—"

"What have we got to lose?" Rudolph shouted, interrupting his father in frustration. "We've been looking three centuries and we're still stuck in these holes!"

"See?" Frederick said to Freda in annoyance.

"This is what comes of contact with mortals. Insolence and disrespect. He's as bad as Gregory!"

"He does have a point, dear," she said, mussing Rudolph's hair affectionately. "Three hundred years is a long time, even for us."

"*Et tu*, Freda?" said Frederick. He turned to Tony and looked him up and down thoughtfully. "And how could a little morsel like you possibly help us in this matter?"

"*Mortal*, dear," said Freda.

"Gee, the Internet, books, school. I dunno." Tony took a deep breath. "But I can try."

"All right," said Frederick. "Help us if you can." Suddenly he pushed Tony back against the wall, his eyes burning like flames. "But do not think to change your mind and betray us to our enemies. If I hear a hint of it on the night air, you will see my wrath revealed! Am I clear?"

Tony nodded mutely.

"Good," said Frederick, stepping back. "Surely you must now go back to your home."

"Be on your guard, little mortal," said Freda, mussing his hair as well. Her fingernails were long and hard and scratchy.

"Umm . . . well, good night, then," said Tony, looking around at the family but unsure exactly how to get home.

"Rudolph may escort you," said Freda, realizing what he was worried about.

"Parting is such sweet sorrow!" said Anna, fluttering her eyelashes. "Good night, good knight, until the morrow!" She brightened. "I know! I'll write you a stirring heroic poem!"

Frederick and Freda watched as Rudolph led Tony away.

"That boy is strange," said Frederick. "A mortal who by his own choice associates with the likes of us. It's unnatural."

"I expect the head-doctors of Vienna have a Latin word for it," said Freda.

"Love for a vampire," said Anna dreamily. "Vampirophilia!"

Chapter 17

Tony and Rudolph walked in silence through the dark corridors, both lost in thought. After a while they came to some ancient stone steps. Clambering up them carefully, avoiding the broken ones that wobbled, they reached the top and peered out through the gnarled roots of an old tree.

Rudolph sniffed the air and listened. "The coast is clear," he said, helping Tony out.

They were in a distant corner of the cemetery. Although it had been interesting, to say the least, to meet Rudolph's family, Tony was glad they were back out in the open air. Instead of damp earth and mushrooms there was the smell of grass and flowers and the sea carried on a salty breeze. Tony breathed deeply.

"I think my father likes you," Rudolph said as they set off for Tony's house.

"That was liking?" said Tony. "He was gonna eat me!"

"Try to understand. He has to be suspicious. Mortals have hunted us for centuries."

"But why? Why do you have so many enemies?"

"Because we're different," Rudolph said grimly. "I mean, we don't harm anybody. People attack us for no reason. It's just a prejudice. It's traditional. Because we are something Other." He sighed. "You have no idea what it's like to be so tormented."

"Oh, yes I do," said Tony, equally grimly. "I have the exact same problem at school every morning."

"You? Why?"

"The other kids think I'm weird because I dream about vampires, and I made the mistake of talking about my dreams."

"You're sure you're not dreaming now?"

"No. This is real."

"What's it like to dream?"

"Don't you know?"

"I can hardly remember. Vampires don't have dreams."

"Then you're lucky. You never have nightmares."

"No. We *are* the nightmare for some people." Rudolph smiled. "What kind of mad person would dare torment Tony, the heroic scourge of Rookery?"

"If you're lucky, you'll never meet such a person." Then Tony suddenly stopped walking, struck by a great idea.

Nigel and Flint were fast asleep. A curtain shifted in the light breeze, and a pair of dark shapes slipped into their bedroom.

Nigel's nose twitched.

A bat shadow passed over his head. His eyes flickered, then opened. The largest, hairiest, most disgusting bat he had ever seen swooped down at him again and again, fluttering in tight circles around the moonlit room.

"Flint!" he shouted. Flint jerked awake and the bat banked and swooped at him. *"Aaaargh!"* he yelled.

The hairy bat landed on the floor, out of sight beyond the end of the bed. Nigel and Flint sat in terror, clutching their pillows. They were unwilling to look at the creature, but they could hear something snuffling and shuffling, grunting and wheezing on the carpet.

"Look!" said Nigel. A head with big ears rose up, silhouetted against the window. It rose higher, revealing a body—but no longer the body of a bat. It had been transformed . . .

The creature seemed to float in the air, like a ghost. It lifted its arms high and said in a low voice: "Wake up, boys. It's party time!"

Nigel frowned. He recognized the voice. "That— that's Tony Thompson!"

It was. Rudolph was sitting on the floor out of sight, holding Tony up in the air by his legs. This was the plan they had hatched to terrify Nigel and Flint. Unfortunately, it didn't work.

"Get the little creep!" said Flint, and both boys tore aside their bedclothes.

Tony toppled backward onto the floor with a clonk as Rudolph dropped him, and his crude bat mask fell off. Time for plan B!

Rudolph jumped up in his place and smiled, a genuine vampire smile, complete with sharp fangs. "Please reconsider," he hissed. His eyes went red and grew big as saucers. To Nigel and Flint, Rudolph seemed to grow, until he towered over them like a skulking, slobbering monster with devil eyes, his shadow filling the room and sucking out all the moonlight.

"I am Tony Thompson's guardian from the Other Side," he intoned, his words dropping like gravestones in an empty hall. "And if you do not treat the Lord of the Underworld with the respect he surely deserves, my teeth will teach you the meaning of pain!"

He leaned forward. "And if you tell anyone about this conversation, you will find yourself on sale in the local butcher shop, minced up small and bagged as rat bait!"

"*Aaargh!*" screamed Nigel and Flint at the top of their lungs, and this time they really let themselves go.

They were still screaming when Lord McAshton burst in a minute later, dressed in his nightgown and cap.

"What's going on here?" he shouted as he switched on the light. The boys clutched each other, terrified. McAshton sniffed the air.

"Now, there's an odor of fear that I haven't smelled for a long, long time," he said.

By then Tony and Rudolph were far, far away.

Chapter 18

When Tony walked into school the next morning, Nigel and Flint were waiting for him as usual. Also as usual, so was a crowd of other children wondering what new entertainment would be performed for them today.

Tony stopped in front of Nigel and Flint, who stood up a little straighter and seemed a bit nervous. The other children looked at one another and stopped chewing their gum. This was unusual stuff.

"Good morning, Tony," said Nigel in a small voice.

"Is there anything we can do for you?" said Flint.

Tony thought a moment. "You know, there is,"

he said. "I need a few books. Perhaps you can check the village library for me and the library up at the manor, too."

"Of course," said Nigel.

"I'll give you a list of the ones I need," said Tony. "But I suppose we ought to get to class."

"Yes," said Flint. "Your bag looks heavy. Shall I carry it for you?"

"That would be cool," said Tony, as he handed over the bag. "You know, I am feeling a little tired today." He yawned for effect. "So much evening work! And I think I might be quite busy tonight, too."

The other children stood open-mouthed as the threesome headed for class.

🦇

Meanwhile, over at his barn, old Farmer McLaughlin opened the doors slowly and carefully.

Sunlight streamed in and hit two cows. They hissed and ran for the shade.

"Cora?" McLaughlin said fearfully. "You, too, old girl?"

He shut the doors again and walked away, as if he hadn't seen them.

Both cows stared at the door, eyes red and fangs sharp.

🦇

It was an important day for Bob Thompson, Tony's dad.

He was in the oak-paneled boardroom of

McAshton Manor, making a presentation to Lord McAshton and several investors in the golf course and convention center. Some of them had come from the other side of the world to see what they were getting for their money.

The presentation was going well. Bob had covered the main features of the conference facilities and had just finished discussing the variety of hotel rooms and catering services. He had saved the best for last—the golf course itself.

Up on the screen he projected a hole-by-hole grand view of the entire course, overlaid with impressive computer graphics showing the ideal lines of attack, the best clubs to use, and various statistics like yardage and pars. The investors were impressed.

"This," said Bob proudly, "is just a small example of the high-tech, multimedia, forward-looking business and leisure environment we are creating here. The future beckons with fingers of—"

Blamm!

The boardroom doors burst open, and there stood an unshaven Rookery in all his finery—leather jacket studded with little metal skulls and ancient feathers, holstered flare gun, big leather boots, and fat, smelly cigar.

In the stunned silence that followed, Rookery surveyed the room with his hard eyes. Lord McAshton, spluttering which indignation, stood up. His monocle dropped out of his eye. "What do you mean by barging in here?" he said.

"I see you're infested with bloodsuckers, my lord," said Rookery.

"I say, old chap," said one of the investors. "I resent that!"

"Vampires!"

"Now, look here—" McAshton began. But then the word hit home. "What was that you said?"

"I said," said Rookery, "you're—"

"Mad!" McAshton shouted suddenly, looking like a startled turkey. "Mad, mad, mad! Obviously barking! I'll have him ejected." With that he ushered Rookery hurriedly out of the room.

Bob and the investors looked at one another in surprise.

"Is he one of those anarchist environmental protesters?" said a woman from Japan, shivering with fear and excitement.

Outside in the corridor, McAshton looked Rookery over appraisingly, but there was genuine fear in his eyes. "Now," he said, "who exactly are you?"

"I am an expert in my field. And in my expert opinion you have here in this parish a virulent nest of the eternal undead."

"You really do mean it."

"Yes. Vampires. The genuine article. They're here, all right."

McAshton took a deep breath and leaned against a wall for support.

"You don't seem terribly surprised," said Rookery. "Should I say instead, the vampires are back?"

"One has heard legends. All nonsense, of course." McAshton pulled out a huge white handkerchief and dabbed drops of sweat off his forehead. "We're, ahh, in the modern world now. Internet, steam engines, and such like."

Rookery stared at him.

"People don't believe in that sort of thing anymore," said McAshton.

"But, my lord," said Rookery with an evil grin. "That sort of thing believes in you. That's what matters."

He leaned close and prodded McAshton in the chest. "And anyway, it's your duty under the ancient laws and charters of Vampyrex Timberens. You as laird are obliged to support my work through denturage, lumberage, and the Pax Fledermaus. To support fang blunting, wooden stake supplies, and the blessings of peace."

"What are you talking about?"

"I'm speaking of my fee."

"Fee? What fee?"

"Without a fee, I can't guarantee that certain things won't start *happening* around here. Know what I mean?"

"Are you threatening me?"

"Oh, no. It's not me who's threatening anyone." Rookery took a deep puff on his cigar and blew smoke in McAshton's face. "So you're refusing to pay?"

"Certainly!" said McAshton, coughing. He suddenly thought of something he had heard about vampires. "Unless . . . have there been any bitings in the area?"

"Bitings? No, not as such," said Rookery, scratching his chin thoughtfully. "Which is odd."

"Well then," McAshton said triumphantly. "There'll be no question of a fee unless I see some proof of your ludicrous claims. Be off with you now before I let slip the dogs." McAshton turned on his heel and walked away.

Rookery's sour gaze followed him. "Typical," he said to himself. "They still think this is some kind of public service."

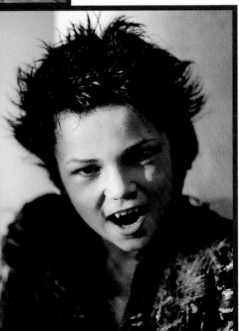

Tony puts on a cape from an old Halloween costume and makes a pair of spiky fangs. He almost looks like a real vampire . . .

. . . but not quite! Rudolph, though, is the real thing.

The little vampire bat flaps his hardest as the truck roars down on him.

Tony can't believe it—he's flying!

"This is just what we're looking for!" Rudolph says when he sees Tony's drawing of the amulet.

Freda and Frederick don't think it's wise for their son to be friends with a mortal.

Frederick raises his cape and hisses like a snake at Rookery.

"Do not think to betray us to our hateful enemies!" Frederick warns Tony.

"I am Tony Thompson's guardian from the Other Side," Rudolph thunders at Nigel and Flint.

Lord McAshton leads Rookery to the abandoned mausoleum.

Anna, Rudolph, and Tony creep down the long dark tunnel from the tomb.

"You're not getting the Stone of Attamon without a fight!" Tony tells Rookery.

Farmer McLaughlin's vampire cows fly through the air, their eyes glowing red.

Tony's parents join the vampire clan at the Gathering.

Frederick lines up the amulet with the moon and the comet, and the ceremony begins.

Chapter 19

Late afternoon found the family Thompson sitting together around their kitchen table. Dottie poured the tea and put a plate of digestive biscuits in the middle of the table.

"I like this, don't you, guys?" she said, but got no answer.

Bob was absorbed in memos and forecasts and planning revisions on his laptop computer. Tony was leafing through one of the fat books of heraldry, crests, and coats of arms that Nigel and Flint had very kindly brought to him at his request.

"Afternoon tea and biscuits. Not cookies. This is all very nice, isn't it?" said Dottie, trying again. "Very civilized. Very English."

"We're in Scotland," Bob said absently, tapping away at a spreadsheet.

"England, Scotland. What's the difference?"

Tony looked up. "The English came from Germany, and the Scottish from Ireland," he said.

"What garbage are they teaching you in that school?" said Dottie, shaking her head. More silence filled the air. "Tony!" said Dottie.

Tony looked up again, furrowed his brow, and remembered something from Nigel's useful note about the Scottish poet Robert Burns. " 'The best-laid schemes o' mice an' men gang aft agley'?" he said.

"I'm no wiser," said Dottie. "This modern slang you young people speak is beyond me. 'Yo, dude!' huh, Tony?"

Tony looked at her blankly. "Oh! One other thing! Mr. Boggins wants us all to look out for Comet Attamon on Saturday night."

"I read that it was called Comet Forsey," said Dottie. "Is this another one?"

Tony ignored her. He had spotted a coat of arms that looked promising. He pushed the book toward Bob.

"Stags are deer with horns, right, Dad?"

Bob barely gave the book a glance. "Deer. Male deer, yes. Lots of Scottish crests have them."

"Lots?" said Tony, disappointed.

"Yeah, means the family was descended from hunters . . . Must show you something. Mmm. . . .

Just a second." Bob spoke into his mini tape recorder: "Idea: Crest with crossed golf clubs for family room."

"Idea," said Dottie. "Why don't we all put down our books and laptops and talk to one another?"

"Okay, sure," Bob and Tony said in unison.

The silence stretched out, and Dottie sighed. Bob returned to rifling through his papers.

"Why are you so interested in crests, Tony?" Dottie asked. "Is this for homework?"

"Umm, it's sort of private project, Mom. If I decide to become Scottish or something I should have plans for my own coat of arms."

"You'll never get to be president if you turn Scottish."

"Here you are! Thought I had it," said Bob. He passed Tony a note from Lord McAshton, written on expensive letterhead. "See? Even Lord McAshton has stags on his coat of arms."

Tony nearly choked on his cookie—biscuit, whatever. His dad had shown him the exact coat of arms he was looking for! The redheaded woman from his dreams must have been a member of Lord McAshton's family!

"Dad, can I keep this?" he said excitedly.

"Yeah. Okay," said Bob.

"And, Dad, can I go to work with you tomorrow?"

Bob looked surprised but pleased. "Tomorrow's Saturday, but sure, I'll be going in. Why do you want to come along?"

"Umm . . . to check out your project, of course. See if I like the design of the golf course, if I'm gonna play on it a lot."

"Great!" said Bob, surprised. "I'll get prepared."

"Will Lord McAshton be there?"

"He lives there, buddy."

"But don't let that stop you, hon," said Dottie.

"Okay!" Tony cheered, and he jumped down from the table.

"Tony," said Dottie, "you've left your—" But Bob raised his hand.

"Let's be glad he's taking an interest in something normal," he said. "There's more than enough weirdness going around as it is."

"What do you mean?"

"My key presentation got interrupted by a big guy who said the village was infested with blood-sucking vampires."

Dottie put her head in her hands. "That's just what we need. Someone's heard of Tony's dreams, and every bum and fringe lunatic is going to come here to see if it's true!"

"Oh, I don't know," said Bob. "This isn't California."

Tony spent the rest of the afternoon in a fever of excitement, eager to get back to Rudolph and his family to pass on the great news. He had discovered the source of the coat of arms, just as he had promised. Now Frederick and Freda would take him seriously, and maybe even Gregory would give him a break.

Tony shuddered to think what Anna might do. Never mind, he had to put up with it.

He paced around his bedroom, wishing the sun would hurry up and set, trying to figure out what he would say when Rudolph came banging on the window that night.

But why wait for them to come to him? It was dangerous for them, after all, what with Rookery hunting them down like a scientist chasing butterflies. He should go to find them instead. He had nothing much to fear. It was time to go solo!

Chapter 20

The last rays of the setting sun were disappearing behind the high trees to the west of the cemetery as Rookery and the caretaker of the church grounds sat around a nice warm brazier next to Rookery's big truck. Rookery had gone up to the rectory and very humbly apologized for the events of the previous night, and invited the caretaker out for a drink. Very civilized, thought the caretaker. Very English.

The caretaker was getting maudlin. "I got no family meself," he said. "No one to be with. All alone in that big rectory till it's sold. Just me and all these dead people." He sniffed and leaned closer to Rookery. "I'll tell you something. My job here makes you think about your own mortality jus' a little."

126

"Really?" said Rookery, looking at the higgledy-piggledy gravestones stretching into the distance. "I would never think of that. You're a very observant man."

"Yes," said the caretaker. "And my conclusion is, you're either a hundred percent alive and full of the joys of spring, or you're dead and six foot under. There's nothing in between." He hiccuped.

"Here's to the alive!" said Rookery.

"To the alive!" said the caretaker. They clinked glasses again and drank.

"And to the dead!" said Rookery.

"To the dead!" said the caretaker. They clinked glasses again and drank.

"And to all the in-betweens," said Rookery.

"To the what?" said the caretaker. He put a finger in the air. "Jus' a minute. I jus' said there ain't no in-betweens. Scientific observation on my part."

"Ah," said Rookery. "I am afraid that's where you're wrong, my friend, though I hate to contradict a learned bod like you. No, there's lots of in-betweens, all different types. Leading a sort of half-life, you could say."

"No! Izzat so?"

"Zombies, for instance."

"Well, now you mention it, I have heard of zombies."

"Your zombie likes the Caribbean."

"Fair enough. So would anyone."

"Good for voodoo and so forth. Ghosts and poltergeists, they like abandoned houses in the more temperate climes, where winters are long and dark."

"I had heard something like that, yes."

"And your werewolf . . ." Rookery gazed into the distance. There was a long silence.

"You were saying?" prompted the caretaker politely.

"Werewolves," said Rookery. "They love the open steppes and plains under the full moon, the wind in their fur, the rhythmic pounding of their paws against the wide landscape, their blood singing in their veins like the music of the heavens!" He sniffed, and the caretaker sniffed, too.

"There was one werewolf I knew," said Rookery, sadly, his eyes misty. "Helga, who ran too fast and too far." His head dropped, and he stared at the ground.

The caretaker looked at Rookery a little cross-eyed. Rookery shrugged. "Anyway, it was not to be. I had my own destiny to follow."

"Aye?" said the caretaker.

"Aye. Vampire hunter."

"Vampire hunter?"

"Vampire hunter. Been in my family for centuries, man and boy."

"That's nice. Keep it in the family."

"Wouldn't have been so bad, except I was the only man and the only boy."

"No!"

"Had to do it all myself. But it was, I know now, my doom."

"Your doom?"

"Destiny. Doom. We each have our own doom."

"Really?" said the caretaker, thinking about it. "Am I also, as you say, doomed?"

Rookery looked at him with hard, glittering eyes. "Oh, yes," he said. "You're doomed, all right."

"Good!" said the caretaker. "That calls for another drink." He poured a generous slug, and they clinked glasses again and drank.

"So you hunt vampires," he said. "What environment do they favor?"

"Cemeteries," said Rookery promptly. "Graveyards and so forth. They seem to prefer the damp places where the dead molder."

The caretaker surveyed his domain, bleary-eyed. "Cemeteries, huh?" he said. "Can't say I've ever seen a vampire here."

"Well, no, you wouldn't," said Rookery, standing up and going over to a rope wound around a winch on his truck. "They're tricksy little blighters. Not many people appreciate the work I do." He tugged at the rope, which started to unwind, with a gentle snick-snick-snick sound. "See, vampires are masters of disguise. Maybe you have seen one, and you just don't know it. You thought you saw a bat, a moth, a cloud of mist."

He absentmindedly made a slipknot at the end of the rope. "Here's a for-instance. They can even transform themselves into something like this rope."

"You don't say!"

"And that is why I am here," said Rookery, sitting down.

He shone his flashlight around the cemetery.

"I am always looking, tracking, listening . . . hunting."

He lurched to his feet, tipping his stool over. "What was that?"

The flashlight beam shone out over the graveyard, hitting the very hole into which Tony had disappeared the night before.

"What was what?" said the caretaker carefully.

"I heard a noise. Maybe I should investigate. Though it would be rude to leave you. You are my guest."

"It's my graveyard," said the caretaker. "I'm the host. It's my job to investititigate. I'll do it." He stood up, swaying.

Rookery held him steady.

"Umm . . ." said the caretaker. "What exactly am I doing?"

"Following a noble calling. You need a steel spine and a steady hand."

"Yeah?" said the caretaker. "Jus' look at this, then!" Proudly he held up one trembling hand.

"Perfect," said Rookery. "You're as ready as you'll ever be. Here, take a safety line."

He put the noose over the caretaker's head and tightened it around his waist.

"Why, thank you."

"And you just follow the vampires into their lair. I'll do the rest."

"Splendid!"

Rookery led the swaying caretaker to the entrance hole.

"Down you go," he said, playing out rope as he lowered the caretaker underground.

Rookery listened for a while before returning to the winch. He wanted to make sure the caretaker was really heading into the corridors and was not just pulling rope down after him.

When he had enough slack, he placed his index finger on the rope and, like an ace deep-sea fisherman, readied himself for a strike.

Softly, he hummed to himself: "Come and get it, my lovelies."

Chapter 21

Far below ground, fast asleep, Gregory hung upside down alongside the other members of his family.

No, not quite fast asleep. His nose twitched. His ears flicked once, twice, like a cat's.

His eyes jerked open. He sniffed the air, alert.

He grinned. He could smell human blood, but not that of Rudolph's stupid friend—there'd be trouble if Gregory bit him, especially now that everyone thought Tony was such a big hero. No, this was a different smell. Riper, somehow. The gamy smell of adult blood. It made Gregory feel alive just to sense it!

And the fool, whoever it was, was heading right into their lair! He deserved whatever he got.

Carefully, Gregory climbed down from his perch and crept from the hollowed-out chamber that passed for a family room in this hole.

Sniffing the air like a bloodhound, he turned left and disappeared into the gloom.

🦇

Rookery was playing out rope as the caretaker slowly moved farther into the catacombs. Rookery's finger twitched gently against the rope, testing the tension.

"C'mon," he muttered to himself. "You know you want it."

Long seconds passed.

And just then—

Thwooommp! The winch started unwinding crazily with a whining noise like a dentist's drill.

Caught by surprise, Rookery fell off his chair. Scrambling to his feet, he made a grab for the rope. "*Aaarrgh!*" he yelled as it burned his hand. Quickly he put on two fireproof gloves, aware all the time that the rope was unspooling out of his control.

🦇

Down below, Gregory ran through the dark tunnels laughing wildly, the caretaker clasped to his chest like a valuable prize. He had done it! He was being a real vampire!

Unfortunately he ran straight past the tunnel in which Frederick and Freda and Rudolph and

Anna, who had just risen from sleep themselves, were standing.

"Greg has somebody!" said Freda, alarmed.

They could all see the rope snaking out behind him.

"Not Tony!" wailed Anna, suddenly scared.

Before they could move there was a loud *thwackkk!* and the rope went taut. Gregory lost his grip on the caretaker and sprawled in the dirt, arms and legs splayed.

Frederick and his family watched in stunned amazement as the caretaker was dragged back past them at high speed, bouncing against the walls.

"He lost him!" Rudolph cried.

Then Gregory scampered past them on all fours like a wolf, a wild animal maddened by his hunger for real human blood.

"Gregory!" shouted Frederick. "Come back!"

But the sounds of the chase echoed through the catacombs. "Stay here," said Frederick grimly. "I'm going after him."

With a rush of wind he disappeared, roaring down the tunnels after his wayward son like a small tornado.

Gregory caught up with the caretaker just as he was about to be hauled up by the rope through the hole and onto the surface. He wrapped his arms hard around the caretaker's legs, desperate not to lose his prize. "You're mine!" he yelled. Together they were pulled up off the ground.

Frederick burst in like a whirlwind and grabbed Gregory. "Let go!" he commanded in a loud booming voice.

Just before they all reached the tiny hole in the earth, Gregory was forced to loosen his grasp, and he and his father collapsed on the floor, panting heavily.

🦇

Tony arrived in the cemetery on his solo mission. He was already regretting his impulsive behavior. What if Rudolph came looking for him and couldn't find him?

But it was too late to go back. He hid and watched from behind a tree as Rookery pulled a dark shape out of the hole and laid it on the ground.

Tony stifled a cry, his heart pounding. Was that shape one of the vampires? But he soon realized it was someone else, someone wearing modern work clothes and not the ornate lacy things the vampires wore. He had no idea who the victim was, and he could not understand what Rookery was doing, but it seemed to be important. Something the vampires should know about, anyway. Tony settled into position, taking care not to make any noise and reveal himself.

Actually, Rookery was concentrating so hard on what he was doing that even if Tony had taken all his clothes off and jumped about on top of the graves singing, he probably would not have noticed him.

Rookery turned the caretaker over and pulled down the collar of his shirt. Then he smiled to himself. There, clearly visible, were two bright red points of blood oozing from a fresh bite in his neck—a vampire bite.

"Ah, my beauties," said Rookery, crowing at his success. "You fell for it! Just a little too hungry, are we? Couldn't suppress that all-devouring desire, eh?"

He pulled out an instant camera and fired off two flash shots that lit up the trees. Then he impatiently pulled out the photos and gazed at the images. "Now I have you! This is the beginning of the end!"

While he was doing that, the caretaker's eyes opened, just a crack. Without making a sound, he slithered off into the tangle of undergrowth before Rookery even noticed that he had gone. Even when he did notice, Rookery didn't seem to be worried.

Tony was more confused than ever. He had no idea what Rookery was up to and why he thought it was such a victory. But Tony knew he could not stay any longer. It was important that he get his information to Rudolph and Frederick as soon as possible, before Rookery got up to any more mischief.

Tony headed cautiously toward the secret entrance he had used with Rudolph the night before.

Chapter 22

Freda, Rudolph, and Anna peered around the corner to where Frederick and Gregory lay in an exhausted heap.

"You fool!" Frederick said to his son. "You bit him?"

"Just a taste," Gregory said.

"Just a taste? Was it really worth betraying your family?" Frederick said bitterly as he got to his feet and dusted himself off. "You've betrayed everything we worked for."

"*I've* betrayed *you*?" Gregory protested, jumping up. He swung his arm out, indicating the dark, damp tunnels. "I've betrayed all this? No, no, *you're* the traitor!"

"What?" thundered Frederick.

"You're the traitor," Gregory repeated. "Forever denying the truth of us. We're lords of the Dark Side, valiant and shining. But you've turned us into feeble cowards, skulking around our holes like earthworms!"

"And what would you have us do?"

"Fight back!" Gregory snapped, displaying his fangs. "Accept the way we are, rejoice in it! Instead of trying to be like mortals, we should make their veins freeze over and pay them back a hundredfold for centuries of persecution!"

"Very eloquent. And you could do it, Gregory," said Frederick. "For a little while. You're young, strong, ruthless. And you're willing to risk a stake through the heart to prove it. For that is surely your fate."

"Better a stake than this plate of ashes."

"For you, perhaps, but what about Rudolph, Anna, your mother?"

"They are with me." Gregory turned to his family. "Raise your voices for once. Tell him we must be true to ourselves."

Rudolph and Anna said nothing, stunned into silence by this outburst.

"Now, dear," said Freda. "Let's not say anything too hasty."

A brief embarrassed silence was broken by Tony running breathlessly into the cavern. "Tony!" said Rudolph and Anna together.

Gregory sneered. "You're happy to see a mortal? What is this nonsense?"

"Rookery's right above you!" said Tony.

"Yes, of course. We must hide!" said Frederick, turning away from Gregory.

"Typical!" yelled Gregory, standing his ground. "Your first thought is to hide!"

"Gregory! Not in front of a mortal!" said Freda, appalled.

"I am trying to protect my family in the only way I know," said Frederick. "You mock my efforts. Do you think me oblivious of your taunts?"

"What does it matter what I think?"

"It matters. And I feel your sting."

"But Rookery!" said Tony, fearfully looking up at the hole.

Above ground, Rookery had stored his photographs and was surveying his arsenal. Emboldened by the success of his last trick, he was going to try something else.

"Let's see if you're still down there, eh, my beauties?" he said to himself as he picked up one of the powerful custom-made ultraviolet antivampire lights that were fixed to the truck. He put on some strong sunglasses, attached the lamp to the winch rope, and lowered it into the hole.

"Let there be light!" he said as he switched on the lamp.

The effect was dramatic. A blazing light filled the cavern, blinding the vampires.

Even Tony found that the brilliant beam hurt

his eyes, but for the vampires it was pure pain that tore into their brains like steel knives. They shrieked aloud as one, a high, alien sound. Rudolph and Anna buried their heads in their mother's skirts. Gregory fell to the ground and whimpered, crawling slowly away from the light. Freda tried to gather her children around her but buckled to her knees in pain.

Only Frederick stood tall, facing the light, his eyes clamped shut, holding out his cape to provide some pitiful shade for his damaged family.

"Run!" he shouted. "Run!" He was taking terrible punishment, visibly weakening as he stood there, defiant. He was unwilling to crumble, though his cape began to smolder and burn, wisps of smoke drifting into the air.

"Come!" Freda commanded, and in the welcome shadow of the cape she pulled her children to relative safety around the corner.

"But what about Father!" Gregory wailed.

"Tony!" Rudolph yelled. "Run!"

But Tony had quickly realized that the light had no bad effect on him.

He knew he had to do something, but what?

Fearing that Rudolph's father was about to be reduced to ashes, he bent down and picked up a hefty rock. Scared but determined, he ran past Frederick and hurled the rock at the lamp as hard as he could. With a crash of glass and a fizzing sputter, the light flooped out.

Welcome darkness rushed through tunnels like a cool wave, and all the vampires sighed an unearthly sigh of relief.

Up above ground, Rookery shivered as he withdrew his broken light. He knew that sound.

"Well, my friend," he said in the general direction of the vanished caretaker. "Very public-spirited of you. You've found yourself a real nest of vipers."

He thought for a moment. "Probably some warriors down there, I'd guess."

As soon as he had his light stowed, Rookery leaped into his truck and drove off into the night, checking his rearview mirrors every now and then to see if anything was following him.

Chapter 23

Underground, the vampires gathered in a quieter, safer, smaller tunnel and tried to recover from their ordeal.

Frederick lay on the ground, badly injured.

"Well, Gregory," he said weakly. "Are you satisfied now? You have brought the very latest weapons down upon us."

"I'm sorry, Father, truly I am," he said as Freda finished strapping him into a straitjacket.

"That may not be enough," Frederick said sadly. "I am damaged. All our hopes are cast down. How can I summon the Gathering of the Clan in this condition?"

"You've gotta keep trying!" said Tony.

"Thank you, little mortal, for the action you

have taken," Frederick said kindly. "But the goal has slipped from our grasp."

"I found out about the coat of arms," said Tony.

"What!" said Rudolph.

"Tony can do anything!" said Anna, her eyes shining with adoration. "He's my hero!" Rudolph elbowed her in the ribs to keep her quiet. "Ow!" she said.

"That's what I came to tell you," Tony said. "The crest is Lord McAshton's. He's my dad's boss. The missing stone must be at his house!"

But Frederick said nothing.

"Did you hear me, sir?" said Tony, worried.

"He is very weak," Freda said sadly.

"What are we going to do?" wailed Anna.

"I know just what you need," Tony said with determination.

Ten minutes later they were all in Farmer McLaughlin's barn.

The vampires shared the remaining three cows. Tony watched from the doorway, disgusted and yet fascinated by the sight. He doubted he would ever get used to it, but at least this time he did not feel sick.

Freda wiped Frederick's face carefully after he had finished.

"Ah, I feel a little better," he said, "though I am still weak. Now I must find a place to hide you children while I find the stone. And then there's the Gathering. I have a busy night ahead of me, I fear."

"No," Freda said firmly. "You're not in a fit state to go gallivanting about strangers' houses. All of us need to rest."

"You can stay at my house," Tony offered.

"Oh, yes, let's!" Anna said excited.

"Out of the question," said Frederick, glancing at Gregory. "Too much temptation . . . and too many windows."

"We've got a cellar," said Tony. "A perfect manchester—plenty of dark space."

"We have little choice now," said Freda as she fastened a muzzle over Gregory's mouth. "The tunnels are too dangerous. Thank you, Tony, for your kind offer. We accept."

She fixed a dog lead to Gregory's straitjacket and handed the other end to Anna. "You take Gregory."

Gregory looked extremely embarrassed at this latest development.

Freda helped Frederick to his feet and dusted him off. "All right, then, Tony," she said brightly. "Lead the way!"

They left the barn and the cows behind and stood outside in the clear air. High white clouds were piled up over the ocean like a fleet of silver sailing ships. The wind was not too strong, great for flying.

Rudolph proudly took Tony by the hand, and they leaped into the sky, followed by Anna leading Gregory, then finally Frederick carried by Freda.

Keeping low to avoid detection by Rookery, wherever he was, the strange formation skimmed over the grassy moonlit meadows and set a course for Tony's house, their hair streaming behind them.

Their departure did not go completely unnoticed. Mitsy, Cora, and the rest of McLaughlin's cows had followed them outside and now watched as the vampires disappeared into the distance.

A dim light of bovine understanding gleamed in their big red eyes.

After a few minutes' cautious flight above the darkened countryside, the vampires approached Tony's house, their capes fluttering.

"It seems very bright," Rudolph said, wincing.

The house was a blaze of light; every room appeared to be illuminated.

"Uh-oh," said Tony. "My bedroom light, as well. I didn't leave it on."

"You mean—" said Rudolph.

"My parents discovered I'm out!" wailed Tony. "How can I explain this?"

"Where are we going, Tony?" said Freda, in a no-nonsense tone of voice.

"There," Tony said, pointing to a small wooden

door set low into the back of the house. A little stone staircase led down to it. "That's the cellar door."

"Good. It seems to be out of the way," said Freda. "You get us settled in and we'll talk."

The vampires slanted down out of the sky and landed on the lawn near the cellar door.

Frederick moaned weakly.

"Shh, now, quiet," Freda said tenderly. "We'll soon be able to rest."

Tony carefully pushed open the door, trying to keep the squeak of its rusty hinges to a minimum. It was dark in the cellar, but Tony did not want to risk switching on the light.

"It's not much, I'm afraid," he said as Rudolph and the others followed him down the stairs.

The cellar was small and cluttered with packing cases from the Thompsons' own recent move and leftover junk from previous owners—crates of books, kitchen implements, newspapers, oil cans, firewood, coal, blankets, flowerpots, and even an old suit of armor.

"Perfect!" Freda declared.

"Is it lightproof?" Rudolph asked.

"I hope so," said Tony.

"We have enough material here to plug any gaps," said Freda.

They heard a clunk and the sound of scraping from upstairs. Tony looked up guiltily. It sounded as if his parents were moving the furniture around in their desperate search for him. They'd be checking under the floorboards next.

"I'd better go up and face the music," said Tony, worried. "I hope I'm not grounded, or else I won't be able to look for the coat of arms."

Chapter 24

Bob and Dottie stood in their living room, worried.

"He's not anywhere in the house," said Dottie. "I'm sure of it."

"I'll just check his bedroom again," said Bob.

"He won't be there!" said Dottie, exasperated. "We've checked and checked."

"This is exactly what happened with Lorna, remember? She said she checked and checked, and then there he was. In his bed!"

"Let's think. He can't have run away. He was in such a great mood. He was looking forward to seeing you at work." She suddenly stopped in shock. "What about that weird guy?"

"What guy?"

"The guy who interrupted your presentation."

"The bloodsucker guy? What about him?"

"You don't think he could be involved?"

"How?"

"Maybe he found out where we live. I don't know. He could have kidnapped Tony."

Bob looked alarmed.

"I'm calling the police," Dottie said firmly.

"It'll take them half an hour to get here. You know what these little country communities are like."

Just then they heard soft footsteps, quiet, measured. . . . And past the door went Tony, his eyes closed, his arms outstretched. He walked slowly and steadily.

"Tony!" shouted Bob.

"Ssh!" said Dottie. "He's sleepwalking. Don't wake him—it's dangerous."

"He even put his clothes on," whispered Bob, marveling. "And look how muddy he got! I wonder where he's been."

With his eyes closed, and with his parents following a good distance behind him, Tony climbed the stairs to his room and slipped into bed, shoes and all.

Dottie put his duvet over him and kissed him lightly on the forehead before leaving the room.

Tony opened his eyes and breathed a sigh of relief. Danger over.

Suddenly overcome by weariness, he fell

asleep, and dreamed of the vampire Von and the strange mortal woman walking hand in hand in the moonlight along the cliffs, smiling at each other.

Sometime in the middle of the night, when all the lights in the rest of the house had been turned off, Tony woke suddenly.

He could sense his door opening and closing softly.

"Mom? Dad?" he called faintly.

Maybe their fears had come true, and Rookery had tracked him down somehow!

His heart thumping, he turned on his bedside light to reveal Anna drifting slowly toward him. She winced at the light, and Tony turned it down.

"Anna!" he whispered furiously. "What are you doing here?"

"I came to see you," she said. She turned around like a model showing off her clothes. There was something a bit odd about the way she looked. Her face was no longer pale; there were two bright red splotches on her cheeks, and her mouth was a gash of red—like blood.

"Are you all right? What's happened to you?" said Tony, alarmed. "You haven't bitten anyone?"

Anna stopped pirouetting and looked down at him crossly. "Don't I look beautiful, Tony?" she said in a hurt voice.

"Well . . ." Tony hesitated. He was unused to

dealing with questions like that, but he had heard about them and knew they could be tricky.

"Is it lipstick?" he guessed. "It looks great!"

"Thank you!" said Anna, preening.

"I didn't know vampires used makeup."

"Well, normally we don't get the chance. But this is the first time I've been invited into a mortal's house for centuries. I had to have a look around."

"What?" said Tony. "You've been walking around the house? Where'd you find the makeup?

Anna waved casually in the direction of the corridor.

"One of the rooms out there."

"Mom and Dad's room!" said Tony, trying not to yell. "Did they see you?"

"Of course not! I know how to tread quietly, like a feather."

"Yeah? Well, you woke *me* up!"

"That's different," said Anna, sitting down on the bed. "You have a special sympathy for our kind, remember? My mother said so herself." Her eyes shone. "Oh, can't you see, Tony? We were meant to be together . . . forever!"

Then she smiled at him, a smile of sharp teeth in bloodred lips, and leaned ever so slightly forward, as if about to bite. Tony shuddered.

"Anna, I really gotta get some sleep. Otherwise I won't be able to help you at all tomorrow. I'll be too tired."

Anna sat up. "I know, I know. But I brought you this!"

From the depths of her clothes she produced a dead mouse.

"A dead mouse?" said Tony, screwing up his face in disgust.

"Take it! It's from the old country. It'll bring you luck."

She put it into Tony's hand.

"And if you ever get in real trouble, just whistle. I'll be your guardian. You know how to whistle don't you?"

She pursed her lips and leaned closer to him, whistling a strange tone softly, not like human whistling at all, more like a call across the wide moors on an ancient flute.

Tony figured he had never been in real trouble until that very moment. But who could he call now? Who could guard him from his guardian?

He puckered up and tried to whistle in reply, but all he could manage was a horrible wet, tuneless, slimy hiss. He had never been much good at whistling.

"Not like that," said Anna. "Like this." And she whistled again. The note echoed and seemed to fill the night with a desolate sound of longing. Miles away a dog barked.

"Wow!" said Tony. "I don't think I can do that."

He was just about to try again when there was a loud impatient banging on the window. He leaped out of bed and ran to open it.

"Rudolph!" he said.

Rudolph looked angry but not with him.

"Anna," he said, "your whistling is enough to wake the dead. Now, come back to the cellar. Tony, don't encourage her."

"Me?" said Tony, but it was too late. Rudolph grabbed Anna and pulled her out of the window.

"Don't forget the whistle and mouse," she whispered as she disappeared from sight.

Chapter 25

With a whoosh the curtains were thrown open again, letting sunlight pour into Tony's room. He opened his eyes and blinked.

He had definitely not been dreaming. He could feel Anna's dead mouse still clutched in his hand. *Euurgh.* He hoped it didn't carry some horrible old disease from Eastern Europe. His teachers in San Diego had warned him about the Black Death, and since he had known he was coming to Europe he had worried about meeting up with it.

"Good morning, hon," said Dottie.

"Hi, Mom!" Tony shouted in guilty surprise. He put his hand under the sheets. He didn't think she would be happy to find him clutching a flea-bitten dead rodent.

155

"Well," said Dottie, "you're as bright as a button today." She looked at him curiously. "We let you sleep late because . . . well. Did you sleep well?"

"Yeah," said Tony.

"Do you remember anything unusual?"

"Yeah," said Tony, deliberately misunderstanding her. "Today's the day I go to work with Dad!"

"Yes. All right. Now, do you want to ask your friend Rudolph?"

"No!" said Tony, a little too loud. "Umm . . . I guess I'll see him later."

"Well, we'd like to meet him and his mysterious parents, perhaps have them for dinner."

"They'd rather have you," said Tony, giggling.

"Whatever." Dottie playfully swatted his rump. "Now, hurry up or Dad will go to work without you."

"Okay." And with that Tony leaped out of bed, still fully clothed, and ran out the door.

Dottie stared after him, shaking her head.

"Tony! You can get changed first!"

🦇

Meanwhile, out in the field, old Farmer McLaughlin was trying to count his cattle.

He did it very, very slowly, as he did not really want to find out the answer. But no matter how carefully he checked every corner of the field, it did not take him long to realize that he had no cows left at all.

Slowly, McLaughlin turned around and faced his barn. Tentatively he walked toward it, every step an effort. And with growing resolve, he pulled open the creaking green door.

A flood of sunlight streamed in, illuminating a scene Farmer McLaughlin would never forget and would never mention to anyone else until the day he died. He saw five cows dangling from the roof beams like so many enormous black-and-white bats, flicking their tails and looking comfortable, with their front legs folded over in front of their faces.

"Sweet mother in heaven!" He shut the door again and strode away, thinking that perhaps next year he would grow wheat and barley or perhaps get out of farming altogether.

🦇

Not very long afterward, while McLaughlin was having a soothing cup of tea in his kitchen, his hands shaking, Bob proudly showed Tony around the grounds of McAshton Manor.

The construction site was impressive: Big yellow machines scraped great slices of turf from the ground. Builders nimbly moved along the high scaffolding that covered the outside of the mansion.

Tony had his eyes open, but he was not really listening to his father droning on about his work.

"The renovation of the building itself is almost

completed. McAshton Manor is pretty old, and over the years some of it has fallen down. As part of the remodeling we—"

"Ahh, Bob, good day," said a cheery voice.

It was Lord McAshton.

Tony looked at him closely, wondering what connection he had with the Stone of Attamon and his dreams.

"Ah, Lord McAshton, let me introduce my son, Tony," Bob said.

"Pleased to meet you," said McAshton jovially, and put out his hand.

"Hello, sir lord," said Tony, unsure how to address an aristocrat.

"Wait a minute," McAshton said. "Aren't you the wacko who stirs up trouble?"

"Tony is interested to hear about your family history, sir," Bob put in quickly. "Especially your coat of arms."

"Really?" said McAshton, suspicious.

"No!" Tony said, alarmed.

"Tony?" said Bob.

But Tony had seen what neither of the others had noticed: Rookery's truck chugging up the drive, its flag fluttering and its engine belching thick clouds of oily smoke.

"It's a bloody history all right," said McAshton. He peered curiously at Tony, who was trying to avoid being seen by Rookery by hiding behind his dad without being too obvious. "You mustn't let it scare you, young man. Now, the McAshton title was created in 1562—"

But he stopped when he, too, heard Rookery's truck grinding to a halt. He turned, and his face went pale.

"I will speak to you later. I have to go now."

He strode toward the truck as Rookery opened the door and stepped down. Bob was baffled—until he recognized Rookery.

"Tony," he said, "stay away from that guy. I swear he's completely crazy. If he comes anywhere near you, make sure to call me or Mom or the police or anyone. . . . Tony? Tony?"

But Tony had gone.

Looking around, Bob saw only Nigel and Flint some distance away, playing cowboys and Indians in the garden. He smiled. Looked like Tony had been distracted by some normal play.

"Ah, Mr. Thompson," said a fat man in a yellow hard hat, the foreman. "Just the bod. We've got a bit of a hitch around the south side. Can you come?"

"Of course." Bob glanced around, saw nothing to alarm him, and walked off as the foreman explained the problem.

But of course Tony was not sneaking up on Nigel and Flint. He had much bigger fish to fry.

He watched from a hiding place behind a rubbish container as McAshton approached Rookery.

"I told you not to come back unless you had proof," said McAshton.

Rookery said nothing. He pulled his two instant photos out from under his jacket and waved them in McAshton's face.

"There's your proof. Vampires attacked the church caretaker and turned him."

"Jamie Davies? Let me see!" McAshton put his monocle to his eye and peered at the images, but all he could see was some grass and leaves. "But there's nothing there!"

"That's because vampires leave no image. No reflections, no photographs!"

"Oh, my good heavens!" said McAshton, suddenly alarmed.

"See?" said Rookery, tracing his finger on one of the photos. "There's a slight indentation . . . an outline of his body."

"I see," said McAshton under his breath. "And he was bitten?"

"The very proof you required," said Rookery. "Two sharp holes in the neck. Not the kind of holes you want at a golf club, eh, my lord?"

"A biting?" McAshton said, in a daze. "Here . . . after all this time?"

"And there'll be more, many more, unless we come to some arrangement."

McAshton looked at Rookery with hard eyes. "What is it you *really* want from me?" he said.

"Now we come to it. Well, there's always my fee, of course."

McAshton waved impatiently. "Done."

"And information. You know more than you admit."

"What do you mean?" said McAshton, insulted.

"Let me remind you. Do you know of any reason why vampires should appear here, of all places?"

McAshton paused. Rookery looked at him closely. "Are there any local connections, perhaps?"

"I never really believed those old stories," said McAshton, his shoulders slumped in defeat. "You'd better come in."

He turned and led the way up the steps and into the ornate hallway of his home. Rookery followed with a triumphant swagger, his flare pistol bouncing jauntily from his belt.

Tony looked around. His dad had gone around the corner and was out of sight. No one else was paying any attention to him, a boy, playing. If only they knew, he thought grimly, how dead serious the game was!

He ran up the stairs into the house. Like a commando on a secret mission, Tony darted from hiding place to hiding place so as not to be caught. He was determined not to lose sight of Rookery and McAshton as they walked through the sunlit corridors of McAshton Manor.

Eventually they came to a heavy door. McAshton pushed it open, and Rookery followed him in. Tony crept up to the door and risked a quick peek inside. Rookery and McAshton were looking up at the walls of a large storeroom, crammed to the ceiling with dusty old paintings of horses and hunting dogs and big stags on the high moors. Above all, it was full of paintings of long-dead McAshtons, dressed in all their Highland finery.

McAshton stood in front of one particular painting and stared at it. It showed a young red-haired woman with a strangely otherworldly expression. She wore an unusual jewel on a chain.

Tony gasped. It was the woman in his dream, the one in the cave, who had laid her cloak on the unconscious body of Von the vampire! And around her neck was the Stone of Attamon!

McAshton was speaking. Tony strained to hear. "It's Elizabeth and her demon lover, isn't it?" he was saying. "They've come back."

Rookery gazed at the painting of the stone, smiling to himself, his eyes gleaming with a quiet fire. This was the stone he, too, had been after for centuries, for his own evil purpose.

"Perhaps you're right," he said. "Tell me about her."

"My grandfather told me the legend. He said it was to die with me."

"That might still happen, eh, my lord?"

McAshton shivered. "She's an ancestor, Elizabeth McAshton. One day while searching for seashells she saw a great sailing ship smashed upon the rocks, though there had been no storm and no reason for the wreck. There was no sign of life. No crew, no bodies. She was a ghost ship. But one survivor had crawled ashore, injured. He had the body of a man—but he turned out to be no mortal."

McAshton paused.

"His name was Von . . . Von Sackville-Bagg. He was a vampire. A crueler and more vicious example of the arrogant vermin you could not hope to meet. And Elizabeth, being a bubble-brained girl, fell in love with him."

"She was bewitched, my lord. He put her under his spell."

"Well, anyway, she was taken by this Von character, and, as legend tells it, she became one of the undead herself, no more to walk in the light of the sun!"

"Then what?"

"The family took measures. Had to." He nodded at another portrait, of a fierce man with a vast beard who stood with one foot on top of a dead stag. "The laird of the manor at the time, old Thunderbreeks McAshton."

Rookery looked at the portrait appraisingly. "And what did he do?"

"Staked her! His own daughter! Staked them both!"

"Warmhearted bunch, aren't you?" said Rookery. "But I approve. It's the only thing to do with the scum. Now, where's she buried?"

"Why do you want to know?"

"Because, my lord, perhaps we wish to discover if it is she who is now walking around, biting innocent people. And if it is she . . . well, if I were a descendant of old Thunderbreeks here, I wouldn't want her out looking for me. Would you?"

He slapped McAshton on the back. "How do you like *your* stake, my lord?"

McAshton paled. "Come with me."

Chapter 26

Rookery and Lord McAshton strode across the grounds at the back of the mansion, heading toward a strange pyramid-shaped building—the abandoned McAshton family mausoleum. It stood alone in its own small clearing deep among the trees, hidden from view of the house like a bad smell. Rookery carried various pieces of equipment—a crowbar, a big flashlight, several hammers—that he had fetched from his truck.

Tony followed a long way behind, running as quietly as he could through the bushes and grasses.

He was making a good job of it, until—

Blam! Blam!

Nigel and Flint appeared right in front of him, blasting away at each other with their toy guns.

"Waaah!" Tony yelled in surprise. Nigel and Flint turned as soon as they heard him. Oh, no! This was the last thing Tony needed. Suppose they alerted Rookery and McAshton. He nearly turned to run off to find his father and give up the idea of searching for the stone.

But Nigel and Flint were screaming. They were more scared of him than he was of them! Tony immediately took advantage. He stretched his arms out with a flourish, as he had seen Frederick do, and yelled as loud as he could: "You're blocking the Lord of the Underworld!"

"We didn't mean to," said Nigel in a small voice.

"That's not good enough!" Tony stood on tiptoe. "I want you to crawl back to your room, get under the bed, and stay there!"

"Yes, Lord Underworld!" The two terrified boys turned and ran away.

"I said crawl!"

Nigel and Flint got on their hands and knees and crawled toward the house. Tony could not afford to hang around to savor the moment. What were Rookery and McAshton up to? He parted the bushes and squinted to see.

They were at the door of the mausoleum. Lord McAshton was nervously trying to open the rusty padlock with a large rusty key.

166

"Allow me, my lord. I am a professional," said Rookery.

McAshton shrugged and handed him the key, but Rookery just leaned back and smashed the door in with one kick of his heavy boot. "All part of the service," he said to the astonished McAshton. They disappeared into the gloom, leaving the door hanging on its broken hinges.

Tony waited as long as he dared before running across the open space after them.

He pushed through the door, wincing as it creaked. What if they heard him? He didn't need to worry. A loud clink of metal on stone echoed around the dark interior; Rookery must have been breaking into something he couldn't just kick to pieces.

Tony let his eyes adjust to the lack of light.

The place was built out of old stone blocks, damp with age and glittering with crystals. Steps led deep underground. Rookery's flashlight beam flickered from down there, shining on the walls and ceiling and revealing gloomy busts of long-gone McAshtons in an eerie light. Tony crept forward slowly, fighting the urge to run away, until he was up against an iron railing at the top of the stairs. He jammed his head between the bars to see what was going on below, careful not to let his glasses fall off.

McAshton held Rookery's flashlight high, illuminating Rookery as he hammered away at the seal of a large stone coffin built into a corner of the room. McAshton was fidgety, making the flashlight dance.

"Keep it still!" Rookery commanded.

"Sorry," said McAshton.

With a final loud smash Rookery broke the last seal. He dropped his hammer and chisel. Then, leaning with all his weight, he pulled the heavy lid off the coffin with a grinding noise fit to wake any dead people underneath.

The coffin was empty. Instead of a body there was just a heap of dry garlic inside a pentagram made of sand. Expensive-looking rings and brooches were scattered about.

"What's the meaning of this?" said McAshton.

Rookery surveyed the scene with his keen vampire hunter's eye. "She's not in her coffin," he said.

"Well, I can see that."

Tony strained against the railing as he tried to see as well. Suddenly the weak bar he was leaning against bent outward, sending him headlong into open space! He twisted and scrabbled with his feet, but he could not keep a grip. He ended up holding on to the bar as he dangled in midair several feet above the open coffin!

Fortunately, McAshton and Rookery were too preoccupied to notice him.

"She must be somewhere else," Rookery said.

"Will she come after me?"

"Perhaps not. I've seen this kind of thing

before." Rookery picked up a piece of dried garlic. It exploded in his hands with a crack like a rifle shot. "Judging by this," he said, pointing at the pentagram, "I'd say she was probably buried here publicly. No point letting superstitious locals find out she was a vampire."

He examined a ring bearing the McAshton crest. "She was then stripped of anything linking her to the family name, like this little beauty. And the body was moved somewhere else."

Tony struggled to keep his grip as Rookery continued. "She'll be in an unmarked grave, wrapped in chains, with a wooden stake hammered through her ribs."

McAshton shuddered. "That's . . . that's horrible."

"Standard operating procedure, my lord." Rookery thought for a moment. "They could not bury her in hallowed ground. But they'd put her somewhere nearby—probably just outside the walls of the churchyard."

McAshton looked into the empty coffin. "You're sure she's not coming back here?"

Just then Tony lost his grip and fell into the coffin in a flurry of arms and legs and dusty garlic clouds.

"It's her!" McAshton shouted, stepping back, terrified.

Tony sat up and coughed.

"Well," said Rookery malevolently, "if it isn't our little day-walker vampire!" He reached for Tony, who bit him in the arm. "Oww!"

"But you're Tommy Thompson, Thompson's son, aren't you?" said McAshton. His eyes narrowed. "The troublemaker!"

"The name's Tony!" said Tony. "And Rookery's trying to—mumblefulb." Rookery had pressed his hand over Tony's mouth.

"Okay, sonny Jim, you've made your bed, now sleep in it," he said. He pushed Tony down into the coffin and slid the heavy lid back on top, trapping him in pitch darkness.

"I say," McAshton said, shocked. "Can you do that? After all, he's just a boy."

"He's one of them. I've seen them all together, slithering about in the night and up to no good."

"But we should tell—"

Rookery pushed McAshton violently against the wall.

"There's plenty of ways to get your throat punctured, my lord." He held a sharpened stake under McAshton's chin. "Don't let me be the one."

"I—I—I . . ."

"You said it yourself. The boy is a troublemaker, a spy for the Dark Side, planning to lead the vampires right to you, no doubt, and—" He drew a finger across his throat. "But I don't expect thanks for saving your life. Oh, no."

Rookery stood back, contempt in his eyes.

"I'm sorry," said McAshton, shaken. He mopped his brow with his enormous handkerchief. "Enemies all around us! I had my suspicions, you know." He looked at the closed coffin. "Is he really . . ."

"Are you safe now? Yes. Now, you'll excuse me. I'm going digging for vampires."

Rookery headed off up the stairs.

McAshton was slow to realize he was being left by himself in the mausoleum.

"Wait!" he shouted, running after Rookery.

Tony was alone in the blackness of Elizabeth's coffin, listening to the sounds of feet echoing away to silence.

All that was left was the sound of his own breathing.

He was in big trouble now.

"Mom!" he yelled.

Chapter 27

The darkness in the tomb was oppressive. Tony pushed at the stone lid with all his might, but it was useless. He would never be able to shift it by himself.

He fished through his pockets and got out his little key chain. He pressed the button, and a tiny light in it glowed red. It wasn't much, but it was better than nothing. Elizabeth's rings glittered, but they weren't any help.

Tony turned out his pockets and looked at what he had. Maybe something could be of use in making his escape. Pez dispenser . . . no. Three coins. Penknife . . . not likely he could cut his way out. Some lint. Anna's dead mouse. That wasn't going to be much use for anything. It was too late to give Rookery the Black Death.

Wait a minute, he thought. What had Anna said? If you need me, just whistle. And then she was going to kiss him. Well, it was worth the danger.

Self-conscious despite the fact no one could hear him, Tony shaped his lips into a circle and tried to whistle. The sound came out again like a mixture of a dribble and a squeak.

"This is crazy!" he said out loud. But at least whistling filled the black silence of the coffin. People always whistled when they were frightened of the dark, to prove that they weren't frightened of the dark. So Tony carried on, trying to remember if he knew any tunes.

Squeak!

What was that? Tony strained to hear. He heard some rustling, then another squeak. An answer? That was quick.

"Anna?" he called as he twisted, trying to locate the source of the sound. He caught a glimpse of two beady little eyes blinking at him from the corner of the coffin.

"Anna, is that you? Are you a bat?"

But no, on closer inspection it was only a mouse, a regular live one. Tony and the mouse stared at each other in surprise. Guiltily, Tony popped Anna's dead mouse back into his pocket.

"I didn't do it, it was given to me," he muttered under his breath, and the live mouse scampered away.

Where had the mouse come from and where could he go?

Tony crawled over to the far corner of the tomb, and what he saw made his heart pound with excitement. One of the slabs of stone that made up the side of the coffin was broken. There was a noticeable draft coming through, too. Air from somewhere outside, probably.

Tony thought for a moment, trying to remember the layout of the mausoleum. This side of the coffin was up against a solid wall—or perhaps it wasn't solid. Perhaps there was a way out!

He just hoped it wasn't a mouse-size one.

Whistling "Yankee Doodle" with confidence but no sense of the tune, he started trying to work the stone slab loose.

Miles way, in the cellar of Tony's house, Rudolph and Anna dangled upside down from the ceiling, sleeping like bats. Gregory was chained to the wall for good measure, but Frederick and Freda lay flat on the floor; Frederick was too weak to get into a proper sleeping position.

Anna's ears twitched. Then they grew bigger, twisting around like radar dishes searching for something. The very thin sound of Tony's whistling called to her.

She awoke, and blinked. It was too early, it was too light. But she had to wake.

She clambered down and went over to Rudolph, shaking him awake, too.

"Rudy," she whispered. "Tony needs us!"

Rudolph blinked. He looked at the window and could see traces of bright sunlight around the edges of the shutter.

"But it's daytime!" he said. "The sun's still up."

"He must be in danger," said Anna. "Or maybe he found the stone!"

Rudolph climbed down from his perch. "Yes, but what can we do now? We have to wait for darkness."

"We can't!" said Anna, biting her lip.

"Hush!" said Rudolph, indicating the peacefully sleeping forms of their parents. "You'll wake them."

He noticed all the junk and clutter they were sleeping among. "Wait a minute. Maybe we can do something, after all."

The noise, despite their efforts, woke Gregory, too. Anna noticed that his eyes were wild and seemed to be pleading.

"I'm not going to let you free," Anna said, wagging her finger at him like a strict teacher. "You'll go and bite Tony, and then think what a mess we'll be in!"

Gregory shook his head vigorously. No! He would ever do that! he seemed to be saying.

"Leave him," said Rudolph, "and help me with this stuff."

Bob Thompson pulled into the driveway of his house, now a little bit concerned about Tony disappearing with Nigel and Flint at the construction site. He wondered how to explain to Dottie that he had temporarily mislaid their son.

But he was in luck. As he got out of the car he spotted something in the distance that could only be Tony on one of his dressing-up days. He looked like a small metal pony prancing across the lawn, heading for the woods. Bob spotted four legs—so Tony must have found a friend—covered in what looked like tinfoil. A deep red blanket hid everything else, apart from a helmet from an old suit of costume armor.

"Hey, Tony!" Bob shouted. But the apparition did not stop, and it soon disappeared into the trees. Bob shook his head.

Dottie came outside. "Hi, honey. Did I hear you call Tony?"

"Yup," said Bob. He indicated the trees. "Just saw him heading there. Seems to have found a friend. Maybe it's that mysterious Rudolph."

"He didn't come back with you?"

"Uh . . . no. I last saw him playing with Nigel and Flint."

"Nigel and Flint?" Dottie's eyes narrowed. "What were they doing to him?"

"Just cowboys and stuff."

"I guess that's good. And you saw Rudolph? What's he like?"

"Well, I didn't see him as such. I got kinda caught up in some problems with the roof. You know how it is."

"But you've just seen Tony back here."

"Yes," said Bob. "It must have been him. Who else could it have been?"

Dottie bit her lips, a little concerned herself.

🦇

Lord McAshton strode through the deserted corridors of his manor house.

"Nigel! Flint!" he called. "Where are you, boys?"

He went into their room and found them hiding under their beds, as ordered by Tony.

"What's going on? Come out of there!"

"We can't!" said Nigel.

"The Lord of the Underworld wouldn't like it!" said Flint.

"Who?" said McAshton.

"Tony Thompson. He's a vampire!"

"But how do you two know about that?" said McAshton as the color drained from his face.

"It was Tony and the other one who came to our room the other night!"

McAshton strode to the boys and pulled them into the open. He inspected their necks for the dreaded sign of two holes. Nothing.

"They didn't bite you?"

"No," said Nigel.

McAshton looked determined. "I have to put an end to this."

"What shall we do?" asked Flint.

"Stay under your beds!" Lord McAshton commanded, and stormed out.

Rookery's truck was parked just outside the church walls. The area was bristling with powerful lamps in preparation for the coming night. Rookery was at the back of the truck, inspecting his drill unit. Everything seemed to be in order.

"Tonight's the night," he said, grinning to himself. He lit a fat cigar and glanced at the sun as it lowered itself into the trees.

He swung the drill arm out and positioned the tip of it on the ground. He flicked a switch, and the powerful motor fired up, spinning the drill bit to invisibility. Carefully Rookery twisted a control wheel, and the drill plowed into the hard earth, digging up dirt and rocks.

Chapter 28

Tony was still working away at loosening the slab in the coffin when he heard a loud whoosh. He looked up.

Suddenly the coffin lid slammed open.

When the cloud of dust had settled, Tony found he was face-to-face with . . .

"Anna!"

She was draped over the lip of the coffin, waving her fan and looking very pleased with herself. "Kiss me, you fool!" she said. She pursed her lips, closed her eyes, and leaned toward Tony. Luckily for him, Rudolph came up behind her and pulled her back. "Tony, are you all right?"

"You *heard* me!" Tony stood up and brushed the dirt off his trousers, avoiding Anna's eye.

"*I* heard you," said Anna. "And I wrote you a poem, as I promised."

"Who did this to you?" Rudolph asked Tony.

"Rookery. We have to find Elizabeth before he does!"

"Well, would you like to hear my poem?" said Anna.

"Who's Elizabeth?" Rudolph asked.

"It's about the power of love," said Anna.

"Elizabeth is the last holder of the Stone of Attamon," Tony said. "The woman in my dream."

"A power that can crack rock," said Anna.

"I think there's a tunnel back here," said Tony excitedly, shining his feeble penlight at the broken slab.

"I recite," said Anna.

"It must lead to her real coffin!"

Anna stood on the edge of the coffin and declaimed: " 'Your face I saw in the ceme-tairy.' "

Rudolph climbed into the coffin with Tony.

" 'Filled with fright,' " said Anna.

"There's a crack here, a hole," Tony said.

" 'For the night was scary.' "

"If we can shift this slab . . ."

" 'But you faced the foe undaunted!' "

Rudolph reached out and with a minimum of effort pulled the heavy stone aside.

" 'It was then I knew, it was you I waunted.' "

"Wow!" said Tony. He peered into the tunnel, shining the pale beam from his penlight into the darkness. "I was right!"

" 'To hold me when the winds are raging.' "

Rudolph turned back to Anna, who had her eyes closed and was swaying from side to side. "Anna, we're going," he said.

" 'To calm my heart when it's rampaging.' "

"Wish we had a better light," said Tony. "I can't see a thing."

" 'To join me in this play we're staging.' "

"Looks fine to me," said Rudolph, peering into the tunnel.

" 'To grow old with me, though I'm not aging.' "

"That's because you're a creature of the night and I'm not," Tony responded to Rudolph.

Anna blasted them both with a powerful flashlight beam.

"Rookery seems to have left this behind," she said. "Now, what did you think of my poem?"

Tony blushed. "Yeah. Ummm, great. I think."

"I wanted to play Juliet, you know. But Shakespeare himself said I was too young." She giggled. "If he had only known!"

Rudolph grabbed the light from her and pulled her into the coffin.

"Don't ever get a sister," he said to Tony. "Especially not this one."

They headed down the long, damp tunnel and into the darkness.

In the Thompsons' basement, Frederick's eyes flickered open, and he saw Gregory bending over him, gently removing the chain and gold circlet from around his neck.

"Gregory, stop! What are you doing?"

Gregory smiled. "Only my duty. I am going to summon the clan."

"But—"

"I know my way to the cliff." He lifted the chain free, wrapped it up, and hid it in his tunic. "I know how to do it. It's better this way, Father. You follow when you can."

With that, Gregory disappeared through the doorway. Frederick, stunned for a moment, reached out and shook Freda. She awoke with a start.

"Well, dearest," she said, "tonight is the night. Mortality or not."

"Gone!" said Frederick. "Gregory's gone with the chain!"

Freda looked up. "The others have gone, too." She smiled. "Although they are ageless, dear one, they are growing up. It is their turn to summon the clan. You should be proud."

Frederick looked around. Sure enough, Rudolph's and Anna's perches were abandoned as well.

"Either Anna and Rudolph let Gregory free or he transformed himself. I wondered how long it would take him to think of that," said Freda.

"But maybe he went to bite a mortal on the way," said Frederick.

Freda put her finger to her lips, to silence him. "Hush. I believe in our children as I believe in you. We have come this far for a reason."

"Your faith is comforting," said Frederick. "We shall go to the cliffs, too. But I feel very weak. I must look a fright."

Freda embraced him.

"You've rarely looked better. And I have known you a very, very long time."

Frederick smiled and squeezed her hand. "Nevertheless, I would fall from the sky if I tried to fly anywhere."

There was a sound from upstairs.

"What's that!" said Frederick, alarmed. "Perhaps Rookery's up there." A worse thought occurred to him: "Or maybe it is Gregory!"

Chapter 29

Dottie was pacing around the kitchen. "It's not like Tony to stay out this late," she said.

"Who knows what's like him these days, ever since he met that Rudolph?" said Bob.

"I thought you liked Rudolph."

"I never really met him. Well, I mean, I did, but he was wrapped in foil."

"Yeah, I know. We've never even seen him."

"We've never met his parents. They're probably foreigners."

"Foreigners? *We* are the foreigners!"

Dottie picked up the telephone handset and started dialing. "I'm calling the cops. Or the coppers, or whatever you call them here."

"Bobbies," Bob said.

At that moment the doorbell chimed.

"I'll get it," Bob said, and he rushed to the front door.

When he opened it, he fell immediately under the spell of the most beautiful and glamorous woman he had ever seen. She was pale and interesting, with hypnotic flashing eyes and a smile of perfectly sharp little teeth that could melt the strongest heart or, if not, slice it into shreds. He could not speak. He had never seen such a gorgeous vision before.

"I am Freda Sackville-Bagg," said Freda in a low, breathy voice.

"That's wonderful," said Bob, in a daze. "You're wonderful! In fact, everything is wonderful!"

Freda blushed and looked him up and down. She breathed deeply and put one hand on the doorjamb, as if to steady herself.

"I'm sorry," she said, fluttering her dainty hand across her mouth. "How rude of me. I haven't been near such a magnificent, healthy, blood-filled adult specimen for a long time." She couldn't help noticing a vein throbbing deliciously in Bob's neck. "The temptation, you must see, the call of the blood . . ." She leaned forward, her mouth opening slightly. "I am so sorry, but our very deepest instinct—"

"Have a care, darling!" Frederick said to Freda as he approached from the shadows. "Remember our vow."

Freda shook her head hard and forced herself to look into Bob's eyes. "It is so strong and it calls to me now, for I am weak." She screwed up her eyes. "But I must be strong. I am Rudolph's mother."

"That's wonderful, too," said Bob again, an idiotic grin on his face.

Freda swallowed and looked away. "I know you're worried about Tony."

"Tony?" said Bob.

"Tony is your son," Freda said.

"We know who Tony is!" Dottie said, coming to the door. "We want to know *where* he is."

"Everything is wonderful," said Bob.

"What's going on here?" said Dottie.

Then she caught sight of Frederick and was immediately as stunned as Bob had been at the sight of Freda. In her glamour-dazzled eyes he looked tall and dark and handsome and dashing, all the things Bob was not. Maybe, like a chivalrous knight, he would throw her over the back of a white horse and lead her away to a better life in the far north, under the icebergs and the stars.

"Tony must have gone to the cliff with Gregory," said Frederick.

"Gregory?" said Dottie, transfixed.

"He's our son," said Bob.

"No," said Freda. "Gregory is *our* son. So is Rudolph. And they've gone with Anna, to see the comet."

"Is Anna our daughter, or yours?" asked Dottie, smiling cheerfully as if she didn't mind one way or the other.

"She's ours, but your son has cast quite a spell on her. He's a natural charmer," said Frederick.

"We think so, too."

"As indeed, so are you, Mrs. Thompson," said Frederick. "Frederick Sackville-Bagg at your service." He took Dottie's hand and bent to kiss it.

It was almost too much for him. To be touching a blood-filled human again, warm and alive, after all these years. Maybe Gregory was right. Maybe it had been foolish to think true vampires could survive on cow blood. What good had it done them, in all those endless centuries? He was weak. He needed proper food! Just one little nibble. It couldn't hurt much.

"Have a care, dear," said Freda, concerned. "Remember the vow."

Frederick kissed Dottie's hand quickly and dropped it. He closed his eyes. That was close.

Frederick and Freda looked at each other and wrapped their capes tightly around themselves. Some of the light seemed to drain from them.

Dottie and Bob found themselves released, just a little, from the fierce grip the vampires' aura had exerted.

"How about it, Bob? I'd like to see the comet, too," said Dottie. "Especially if Tony is there," she added as an afterthought.

"Sure," Bob said, shaking his head. "Do we have to be in fancy dress?"

"Fancy dress?"

"You know, the Shakespeare-aristocrat costume deal."

"This is not a costume, as you say," Frederick replied coldly. "We are aristocrats and entitled to wear our own clothes!"

"Please hurry," said Freda. "It's urgent." She looked up at the full moon rising, and sure enough the comet was close to it.

"Right . . . Where's your car?" said Bob.

"We flew," said Frederick before Freda could stop him.

"I am sorry. My husband is not well. We'll have to go in your carriage," said Freda.

"Of course."

Just as they were about to clamber into the Land Rover, Lord McAshton's old Bentley roared into the driveway and skidded to a halt.

McAshton shoved open the door and fell out of the car in his excitement. He picked himself up off the ground and trotted breathlessly over to Bob, carrying an ax and a stake. Frederick and Freda shrank back into the gloom at the sight of that hated combination.

"Hold up, Thompson, old boy!" said McAshton. "I've got a job for you! You won't like it at first. We McAshtons didn't like it three hundred years ago, when we had to do it. But we did our duty. That's the point! Duty!"

McAshton became very matter-of-fact, demonstrating how to hammer in a stake.

"Place the point of the stake over the heart. Use the blunt end of the ax. Tap-tap-tap. It has a nice rhythm. Tap-tap-tap. One, two, three—spurt! It's all over. Trouble gone."

"What on earth are you talking about?" said Bob.

"You have to drive this stake through Tony's heart!"

"Oh, my God!" said Dottie. "Are you completely insane?"

"Don't worry. He's already dead. He's a vampire!" McAshton leaned close. "It can't be easy for a father to hear this, but your son's nothing less than a bloodsucking fiend."

McAshton held out the ax and the stake, and smiled. "Take them. You'll thank me in the morning."

Bob pointed a finger right in McAshton's face. "I have had it with you and all this vampire trash. Don't ever, ever, ever call Tony a vampire again. How dare you embarrass me and my wife in front of our guests. These people"—he hooked a thumb over his shoulder at Frederick and Freda—"are real, genuine aristocrats! A proper lady and gentleman!"

"Real aristocrats? Well then, they'll know all about duty!"

Frederick stepped forward out of the shadows, supported by Freda, and stared balefully at McAshton.

"My lord, we know Tony, and I can guarantee that he is no vampire. Now drop that ax and take your leave, sirrah, or there will be turmoil between our two houses."

McAshton wilted under Frederick's power. He dropped the heavy ax on his foot without even feeling it.

"Yeah, take your leave, or you'll be building your own golf course," said Bob.

McAshton tossed the useless wooden stake over his shoulder. "All right. I'm leaving." He staggered back toward his Bentley.

"Did you hear that, Dottie? I told him to take his leave," said Bob.

"You were wonderful."

"Please," said Freda. "The comet."

Bob opened the doors to the Land Rover. Dottie helped as Frederick and Freda got into the backseat a little cautiously, as though they had never been near a car before. Then Dottie climbed in and Bob fired up the engine, put the car into gear, and drove off down the drive.

"You should be ashamed of yourself!" he yelled at McAshton as they passed the Bentley. "You shouldn't be driving in your condition!"

McAshton was left sitting there in his car. He thought back over the events of the evening and the few days before and tried to work out what had gone wrong.

Then he realized . . . "Those people weren't aristocrats. They were vampires!"

In the Land Rover, Bob adjusted the rearview mirror. What he saw—or rather what he didn't see—shocked him.

There was no one in the backseat!

Quickly he looked over his shoulder. Frederick and Freda were there all right, sitting bolt upright in the back, clearly uncomfortable.

"Is something wrong, honey?" Dottie asked.

Bob just shook his head.

Chapter 30

While their parents were getting to know one another and heading down moonlit country lanes together, Anna, Rudolph, and Tony were creeping cautiously down the long dark tunnel from the empty coffin in the McAshton mausoleum.

The sound of their own breathing and the tread of their feet and the drip-drip of water coming from the damp roof was all they could hear. It seemed as though they had been underground for ages and had been walking forever, but as far as they could see they had not gone anywhere at all.

The walls looked the same. The floor looked the same. Behind them the tunnel curved around a corner and into darkness, and ahead of them it curved around another corner and into more darkness. Cobwebs and the roots of trees hit them in the face from time to time, even though they had the flashlight to light the way.

And every now and then there was a distant sound, a whine like a dentist's drill vibrating through the rock.

"What's that?" said Tony.

"I'm not sure," said Rudolph. "But it doesn't sound good."

Anna tripped over a big stone.

"It's very uneven," she whispered crossly.

"I suppose it was dug in a hurry and only used once," whispered Tony. "From what Rookery was saying, we're lucky it hasn't fallen in."

"Maybe it would be better if it *had* fallen in," whispered Anna.

"Then we couldn't get through," said Rudolph.

"Yes, but now the tunnel might fall in on us while we're in it! If it had already fallen, we would be much safer," said Anna with impeccable logic.

"Ssshhh!" said Rudolph.

"Why are we whispering?" said Anna.

"The walls have ears, you know," said Rudolph. "That mouse Tony saw—who knows who he was working for."

"We must be near the cemetery by now," said Tony.

"You've been saying that for hours!" Anna complained.

"It hasn't been hours, Anna," said Rudolph. "Don't exaggerate."

"Something feels different here," Anna said suddenly.

They all stopped. "I agree," said Rudolph. "It's as though there's more air . . . and the echoes sound different."

"I don't notice anything," said Tony, shining the flashlight ahead. The beam made weird shapes out of the dangling roots. He was glad he was down here with his friends and not all alone. But it would be better still to be out of the tunnel.

"Let's get moving," he said, and hurried off around the corner.

"To the ends of the earth, darling!" cried Anna as she and Rudolph followed him.

But then they could go no farther. They slammed to a halt, panting and gasping in pain. It was as though a solid wall had risen in front of them.

"What's wrong?" said Tony. By this time he was several yards ahead.

"Something ahead," said Anna.

"Something accursed!" said Rudolph. "A holding spell."

"You'll have to go first," Anna told Tony.

"Are you okay?" Tony asked, worried.

"Yes, if we keep back. Find out what it is," Rudolph said.

Rudolph and Anna scrabbled back a few feet,

until they could no longer feel the spell's weight on their hearts. They leaned against the wall of the tunnel, watching.

Tony felt very uncomfortable and alone. What if something happened? They wouldn't be able to rush to his aid. He was on his own. But that, after all, was why he had offered to help the family, to go places where they couldn't. He had expected that to mean sunlight, of course, and not a damp tunnel. But he had to do what he had promised. He pushed ahead.

Now he, too, could feel the air change. There was a change in the quality of the sound.

"The tunnel opens out into a bigger space," he called out, "like a room carved out of the rock, and— Wow!"

"What is it?" cried Rudolph.

"I think we found it!"

"I knew you'd save us!" said Anna, clasping her hands together.

Tony's flashlight beam shone on a huge stone sarcophagus swathed in chains. He moved forward to take a closer look. The stone coffin was big enough for two, and the lid looked heavy. The chains, too, were massive, hefty enough to moor ships. And they were secured by a fat rusty padlock that sat on top of a stone tablet on the lid. The tablet carried an inscription.

"There's something written here." Tony brushed

away the dust of centuries. "C-A-V-E-A-T V-A-M-P-T-O-R. What does that mean?"

"It's Latin," said Rudolph. "*Caveat vamptor*—let the vampire beware. That's the curse!"

"Oh, how you mortals taunt us!" wailed Anna.

"Not all of us," said Tony grumpily.

"Of course, my dearest. How thoughtless of me."

Tony stared at the padlock. How was he going to break into that? But maybe it had rusted so much that one blow would smash it.

He picked up as large a rock as he could hold in both hands and pounded away at the padlock.

Nothing happened.

"I can't do this!" he yelled.

"Courage, darling!" Anna cried.

He tried again. "Stupid thing, break, break!"

But the padlock held. It was as strong as the day it was locked. Tony knew he would never be able to smash it. He would pound the rock to powder before he broke the lock.

"It's no use!" he called out in despair, dropping the rock. "We need a miracle!"

Just then they all heard the mysterious whine vibrating through the ground. It sounded much closer and deeper.

"There it is again," said Rudolph.

"It seems . . . It seems to be coming from right above me," said Tony.

He looked up. The roof looked exactly as it

must have looked for years, centuries even. Or did it? It was vibrating. Dust started falling from it. The noise got louder and louder.

Suddenly a spinning metal tip tore through the rock, and a torrent of earth and dust and little stones burst out like a small tornado.

Tony covered his eyes with his arm and scrambled behind a pillar.

"Oh, no!" cried Rudolph.

Carefully, Tony peered out. A huge drill was spinning down, heading straight for the coffin. "Yes!" he yelled happily. "We got our miracle!"

He darted out of cover and pulled the padlock over so it was directly under the drill bit, then scampered back to safety.

The drill came closer, closer. Then, with a shower of sparks and screeching like a banshee, it smashed into the lock and wrapped the chains around and around itself. The drill continued on down and shattered the stone tablet. At the same time the padlock snapped, and with a rattle the chains fell free.

Then the drill itself broke apart. Heavy lumps of metal zipped through the air and clanked against the walls. Whoever was controlling the drill immediately shut it off, and it slowed to a halt. Smoke and dust swirled about in little whirlwinds.

"We're free!" yelled Anna.

"You've done it! You broke the spell," said Rudolph, relieved, as they came up to Tony.

"It must be Rookery," Tony said, worried, as the sad remains of the drill were slowly lifted back up through the hole. "Quick, help me raise the lid. We have to get the stone before Rookery realizes we're here."

With Tony's help, Rudolph and Anna pushed and pulled at the heavy stone lid. Finally, with a loud, echoing grinding noise, they managed to push the stone coffin open.

Tony gasped. In the coffin lay a man and a woman in ancient clothes. They looked as if they had just gone to sleep—apart, that is, from the stakes hammered into their hearts.

"That's Elizabeth," Tony said. "She looks just like her picture and like I saw her in my dream."

"And that's Uncle Von," Rudolph said sadly. "Father was right."

"But how romantic!" said Anna. "Their love preserved forever."

"Uh-oh," said Tony, pointing at Elizabeth's neck. The chain she had been wearing in the portrait was around her neck all right, but a key item was missing. "The Stone of Attamon—it's not here!"

"Maybe it fell off," said Rudolph hopefully, checking the gloomy innards of the coffin.

Tony, as if mesmerized, reached for the chain instead. As soon as he closed his fingers around it—*puff!*

The dry bodies of Elizabeth and Von burst into clouds of choking dust.

"Oh, Tony," wailed Anna as she saw the remains of her romantic hero and heroine drift away on the air currents. "What have you done?"

But Tony could not hear a word she was saying. As soon as he had touched the chain he felt a deep chill on his heart, as though he'd been plunged into Arctic waters.

"*Aaaaaah!*" he shouted, but he couldn't let go of the chain.

"Tony!" Rudolph shouted, as Tony's eyes rolled back in his head. He was shaking uncontrollably as he was thrust into another vision.

A castle on a hilltop, silhouetted against the sky. Two people running, chased by twenty or more others, carrying torches and pitchforks and spades. Tony gasped. The castle was his house, but it looked different. It looked like a real castle.

And the people running—they were Elizabeth and Von themselves, running desperately from a group of fierce and angry villagers led by Lord McAshton! But it was a different Lord McAshton. Tony knew it must be his ancestor Thunderbreeks McAshton.

Tony watched helplessly as Von turned to face the villagers, sending Elizabeth ahead into the castle. Crying, Elizabeth saw Von get caught by the mob, brought down, and lost in a frenzy of fighting.

Thunderbreeks caught sight of her and pointed, and the mob followed. Elizabeth turned and ran, clutching the Stone of Attamon. She ran inside the castle and up a winding staircase, kicking aside windblown leaves. Heavy footsteps echoed behind her. Wild-eyed with fear, she ran down a corridor and darted to her left, into a small room.

Tony recognized it: his own bedroom, hundreds of years ago! Elizabeth slammed and bolted the door. Glowing torchlight flickered around the edges.

She stepped backward fearfully as the frenzied villagers pounded on the door. She had nowhere to go, nowhere to hide. She stumbled on a loose board and fell to the floor.

Under the boards, there was space. Desperate, she took the precious Stone of Attamon from the chain around her neck, stuffed it hurriedly into her bonnet, and dropped it into the dark hiding place. She managed to replace the board as the door burst open and Thunderbreeks strode in, grimacing in disgust. He raised a cross.

Elizabeth hissed her defiance, but to no avail. Thunderbreeks stepped forward, and everything went hazy.

Tony opened his eyes.

"Are you okay—"Anna began, but Tony interrupted.

"No wonder I had all those dreams!" he shouted, a look of revelation on his face. "The stone was right near me all that time!"

"What?" said Rudolph and Anna together.

"Elizabeth hid it by my bed," said Tony.

But instead of being excited by this, Rudolph and Anna suddenly froze and looked up into the distance.

"The call," said Rudolph dreamily.

"We must go," said Anna.

"Yes," said Tony. "We have to go home."

But Rudolph and Anna were paralyzed. What was going on? Tony waved his hands in front of Rudolph's face. Nothing.

Helpless, Tony looked around him and noticed something dangling from the drill hole: a microphone. What was that doing there?

"Oh, no!" said Tony, suddenly aware. "Rookery! He heard everything!"

Mocking laughter seemed to echo down from the surface. Then came the familiar growling of the big truck engine firing up.

"He's going to get there first!" said Tony, pulling on Rudolph's arm. "Wake up!"

"It's the call," Rudolph said again, as if that explained everything.

"Yes," said Anna. "We have to go to the Gathering . . ."

"What are you talking about?" Tony shouted.

Rudolph looked down at him coolly, as though he was a stranger. "It is the Calling for the Gathering of the Clan. We are summoned, and we must go."

Before anyone could say anything else, Anna rose off the ground and flew out through the new drill hole.

"Anna!" yelled Tony.

"I must go with her, Tony," said Rudolph. "We are all called."

Chapter 31

It was true. The Gathering of the Clan of Sackville-Bagg was well under way.

On the edge of a high cliff overlooking the deep black ocean, alone beneath the full moon and the stars and the comet, Gregory stood, proudly swinging his father's gold circlet on its chain in wide, glistening circles.

A low hum, audible only to vampires, emanated from the spinning chain and vibrated through the ether, calling to those who could hear.

Across the sky, many strange bats also heard the sound, and plunged on through the air, singing a song at a higher pitch than humans could hear.

Mr. Boggins, Tony's teacher, could not hear the

…d, but as luck had it he was out on his terrace with his telescope set up to look at the comet and the moon. He was extremely surprised to see the sky filled with bats.

He stood up and mopped his brow.

Frederick and Freda, hurrying down the road toward the cliffs in the Land Rover with Bob and Dottie, also looked up.

"Do you hear it?" said Freda.

"Hear what?" said Bob.

"Gregory?" Frederick said.

Freda nodded. Then she put her hand on Dottie's shoulder. "Whatever you see tonight, do not be afraid. Though some may be tempted, we'll let no harm come to you."

"What are you talking about?" said Dottie. "What harm?"

"None," said Frederick. "You should be fine." But he seemed a little worried as he looked at his wife.

In their field, the herd of vampire cows could also hear. They looked up and then at one another.

Wise Mitsy closed her eyes and bowed her head, and with a loud "Mooo!" she led her comrades out of their field and to their date with destiny.

Down by Elizabeth and Von's tomb, Tony was having a hard time keeping Rudolph's attention.

He had grabbed him by both arms and was trying to stop him from flying away after his sister.

"Snap out of it, Rudolph!" yelled Tony. Then he did something he thought he would never do. He slapped Rudolph hard across the cheek.

"Ow!" said Rudolph. He looked at Tony angrily, as though he had been woken from a happy dream. His eyes focused. "Tony!"

"What's up with you?" said Tony. "We've gotta get to my house!"

"The stone!" said Rudolph. "I'd forgotten!"

"How could you forget? And what's all this about a Gathering?"

"There's no time to explain that now. Let's go!"

He grabbed Tony's hand, and they took off.

It was a hard squeeze following Anna up through Rookery's drill hole. Halfway out, Tony was painfully scratched by little stones and twigs trapped in the earth.

Near the top he got jammed. For a wild second he was scared he would be stuck there for ever.

"Breathe out!" Rudolph called, and Tony exhaled as much of the air in his lungs as he could. Pulling and pulling, Rudolph finally popped him out of the hole like a cork.

Tony crouched on his hands and knees, panting like a dog, and looked around. No sign of Rookery, but the grass looked as if it had been attacked by an army of enormous moles.

"Wow!" said Tony.

"Rookery was drilling for information. He made Swiss cheese of the area." Rudolph looked down at Tony. "Are you all right?"

"Yes, better now. Got my breath back. Rookery must be halfway there by now."

Rudolph held out a hand.

"Well then, let's stop him!"

Tony grabbed his hand, and the two friends leaped into the sky and soared off into the darkness.

Atop the cliff, Gregory had completed the summoning. He was holding his father's gold circlet and chain when Anna arrived.

"Hello, Anna," he said. "You're the first."

"Hello, Gregory," she said, smiling.

The noise of an engine made them both turn. The Land Rover drove up and parked thirty yards from the edge of the cliff.

"I don't see Tony here," Bob murmured to Dottie.

Frederick and Freda leaped out and strode to where their children stood on the cliff. Bob was about to get out, too, but Dottie stopped him, allowing the reunited family this private moment.

Above the choppy sea, the moon looked big and forbidding. The Comet Attamon looked as if it was almost touching the moon.

"It's almost time," said Frederick, laying a hand on Gregory's shoulder. "Thank you, son."

Gregory smiled up at him.

Freda looked around. "Where is Rudolph?"

Anna thought for a moment, her brow furrowed. "I do know." Then she brightened. "I remember. The Stone of Attamon is in Tony's bedroom. He and Rudolph must have gone to get it. I would have gone, too, but it was such a beautiful summoning that I had to come."

"As did we all," said Frederick, looking up into the sky.

In the Land Rover, Bob and Dottie were just about to get out to join Frederick and Freda when something amazing stopped them.

"Oh, my God," said Dottie, alarmed.

People, real people, were dropping down out of the sky! They landed on the cliff and by the wood and in the grass and all around the car.

They were weird people, dressed in fantastic outfits, with long hair that burst from their heads or was piled high in bizarre styles that were definitely not the modern fashion. They were vampires from across the centuries, members of the clan of Sackville-Bagg.

"This *is* a fancy dress event," said Bob. "How did they do that?"

Some of the new arrivals noticed them and gathered around the car curiously. They all had pale faces and dark eyes, and some of them were licking their bloodred lips.

"I don't think those are costumes," said Dottie. "These people look . . . real."

One of the newly arrived and very real vampires—Otto van Bleek was his name—smiled, revealing gleaming fangs.

"How very thoughtful of Frederick!" he declared to his wife, Eleanor. "A last little snack before our journey."

"Uh-oh," said Bob.

"Freda promised we'd be safe," Dottie said, sounding doubtful. "I wonder what she meant."

The van Bleeks and other vampires were suddenly pushed aside by Gregory.

"These people are our friends," he said to them. "You're to leave them alone."

"Thanks, Rudolph!" Dottie called. "You must be Rudolph?"

"No, I am afraid not," said Gregory, looking worried.

"Then where is Rudolph?" said Bob.

"And where is Tony?" said Dottie.

Chapter 32

Tony and Rudolph screamed in over the trees like a pair of fighter jets and clattered to a rough halt on the little balcony outside Tony's window.

"Wow!" said Rudolph. "That was my hardest landing yet!"

"Hurry!" said Tony.

"Normally you're inside and you open the window for me!" Rudolph declared.

"But hurry anyway!" said Tony. "Rookery's coming!" He was looking out over the dark landscape. The deep growl of Rookery's truck was easy to hear. It couldn't be far away, just beyond the hill now, only a hundred yards away perhaps.

"But I don't know how to open the window!" said Rudolph.

Tony grabbed it and pulled it open.

Suddenly lights flared as Rookery's ultraviolet vampire-killer lamps blasted at the house.

"The light!" Rudolph wailed. Tony pushed him inside and tumbled in after, landing on top of him. The blazing rays lit up the inside of Tony's bedroom like white fire.

"Quick!" said Tony.

Rudolph crawled away from the window, desperate to keep below the rays. Then they faded.

"Good! They've stopped," said Rudolph, breathing easier.

"That's only because he's parked. He hasn't gone away. He'll be up here soon."

"All right, Tony. Now, where is the stone?"

Tony looked around his room, desperately trying to remember where he had seen Elizabeth place the stone. But everything was a little bit different now, of course. Different bed, different door, different fireplace. The old oak wardrobe was the same, though.

Tony pulled up a rug and threw it onto his bed. All the floorboards looked alike!

"Here, I think," he said, and tried to pull one up. Rudolph knelt beside him, a look of eager expectation on his face.

But they couldn't shift the floorboard at all.

Outside, Rookery clambered out of his truck with slow deliberation. He dropped the butt of his cigar and ground it into the mud under his leather boot. A grim expression on his face, he pulled out a heavy sledgehammer. He meant business now.

He strode purposefully to Bob and Dottie's front door, which, as he expected, was locked. He stepped back, lifted the hammer, and swung a huge blow.

Boom! The sound echoed in the night air. Rookery smiled. The heavy oak door cracked but did not give way.

Tony heard the sound and panicked. "He's here!"

"Not yet. We can still do it!"

Booomm!

Tony spotted another floorboard. "Maybe it was this one!"

Boooommm!

"We need something to pry these boards up!"

Booooommmm! Crash!

The front door gave way, and Rookery stepped through the smashed portal and into the hallway, a vicious grin fixed to his face. "I'm coming, ready or not!"

"I've got it," Tony yelled as he pulled a wedge iron out of his new golf bag. Eagerly he jammed it between two floorboards and pushed down. With a squeak of protesting nails, the board popped up.

Rudolph grabbed and tugged. The floorboard came away easily—but nothing was hidden in the rubbish underneath.

"Try the next one," said Rudolph.

They could hear Rookery's deliberate steps echoing on the stone staircase as he ascended steadily, looking around him, aware of the dim possibility of some sort of a trap.

"He's almost here," said Tony, as he pried up another board.

"There's nothing here," said Rudolph. "Try this one."

Rookery's boots creaked noisily as he marched down the corridor.

"Stop him from getting in," said Tony in sudden desperation.

Rudolph jumped up and looked around for some means of barring the door while Tony continued to jimmy up floorboards. The only thing Rudolph could see that might hold Rookery back was Tony's heavy wardrobe.

He got between it and the wall and pushed with all his might. Slowly, scouring deep scratches in the floor, the wardrobe moved inch by inch until it stood in front of the door.

"That gives us a bit more time," said Rudolph. "Have you found anything?"

"No," said Tony, close to tears. "It must be here somewhere," He pulled up another board. "I don't have time to go to sleep to see what happened next."

Rookery stopped outside Tony's bedroom door and listened for a second to the sounds of activity.

He tried the handle. The door opened but clunked immediately into the wardrobe.

"Oh, dear, you've blocked the door," he said, hefting his sledgehammer again. He swung it back and smashed it into the wood. It split but not enough to get through.

Tony lifted up one more board; Rudolph pulled it back. The two boys were tiring now, but they struggled on.

A crash and the sound of splintering came from the doorway.

"Here! I think I've got it!" cried Tony, dropping the golf club. He scrabbled in the dirt under the floorboard and pulled up Elizabeth's bonnet. Quickly he unwrapped the ancient, moldering material.

Inside it gleamed a deep red ruby.

"The Stone of Attamon!" breathed Rudolph. "Let's go!"

Crash! Too late. The bedroom door gave way.

Rookery smashed through and burst out through the door of the wardrobe, some of Tony's T-shirts draped around his shoulders. He just caught a glimpse of Tony hiding the stone in the bonnet and jamming it under his shirt.

"Get out!" yelled Rudolph in a shriek, like fingernails on a blackboard.

Rookery dropped the sledgehammer and drew out his trusty electric cross. Rudolph squealed at the brilliant light and was hurled back into the fireplace.

Tall and terrifying in the strange light from his cross, Rookery stared down at Tony. He grinned triumphantly. "It's all over now, boy. Hand the stone to me!" he commanded, extending one enormous callused hand.

"No way!" said Tony.

"That stone belongs to me," said Rookery. "Give it to me!"

"It belongs to my friends."

"Friends, ha! Those bloodsuckers! They use you and then they discard you." Rookery leaned closer. "Don't be a traitor to your kind. Give the stone to me."

"Not without a fight," said Tony, defiantly.

"I really can't be bothered," Rookery said. He stepped forward and picked Tony up, bonnet and stone and all, and tucked him under one arm.

"Let me go!" yelled Tony, kicking his legs, with no effect. Rookery strode to the window and stood on the balcony. Tony was pretty sure Rookery couldn't fly, so what was he going to do next?

In answer, Rookery pulled out a fat pack from a pocket. Holding it with one hand, he pulled a toggle with his yellow teeth, then dropped the pack to the ground far below.

It hit and suddenly inflated with a loud pop, forming what looked like a bright orange bed. Suddenly Rookery and Tony were in the air, falling, falling—bounce!

Tony felt as though his stomach had rammed into his throat. This was far worse than flying.

Rookery hauled him to the truck, tossed him into the cab like a sack of potatoes, and clambered in himself. With a clash of gears he pulled out, spun the steering wheel, hit the accelerator, and drove out through the gates, whipping up gravel as the truck picked up speed.

Now that Rookery and his painful electric cross had gone, Rudolph was able to crawl out of the fireplace. He got to the window just in time to see Rookery's truck reach the main road and pull away, all its lights on.

"Tony!" he called in despair.

What now?

Chapter 33

Rookery's truck sped down the narrow roads, its blazing antivampire lights shining on the trees and hedges, and lighting up the night sky.

In the cab, Tony still had one hand jammed up inside his shirt, fist tightly clenched around the stone. Rookery had one meaty hand on the steering wheel, one holding Tony in place. Tony wriggled and squirmed, but it made no difference.

"Give it here," Rookery ordered.

"No."

"Whoa!"

Rookery suddenly had to concentrate on driving. A herd of cows was walking in single file up the road, toward the cliffs.

"What are you doing out this time of night?"

Rookery yelled angrily, blasting the horn as he pushed past. The cows, spooked by the noise, skittered nervously over to the side of the road and let the big truck pass by. As its taillights disappeared around the corner, one cow's red eyes gleamed in annoyance—Mitsy's.

Rookery got back to business. "What were we talking about? Ah, yes, the stone. Now you can give it to me, young man." He grabbed Tony's arm and pulled his hand out from beneath his shirt. There in Tony's fist was his prize. Rookery's eyes glinted.

"My friends need that stone," Tony wailed.

"To enslave us all," Rookery shouted. "Don't you know the vampires are the bad guys and the vampire hunters are the heroes?"

"No."

"And I need the stone, laddie, to send those fiends to hell."

"No!"

But it was no use. Rookery was too strong. He pulled Elizabeth's bonnet out of Tony's protesting grasp. Still steering with the other hand, he flipped it open and saw the stone, sparkling in his palm.

"Ah!" he said.

He glanced up at the road. "What the—" Something was floating a few feet above the roadway a hundred yards or so ahead.

Rookery wrapped the stone again and shoved it

on top of the dashboard. He hit the brakes hard, using both hands for steering. The truck skidded to a halt in the middle of the road, smoking like an angry dragon.

Rookery peered ahead into the night.

"Rudolph!" said Tony, then clapped his hand over his mouth. Oops!

Rudolph was floating in midair, out of the range of the antivampire lights, smiling and waving.

"What's he playing at?" said Rookery suspiciously.

As if in answer, a large black-and-white cow drifted down out of the sky and took up a position just behind Rudolph, hovering above the road. Mitsy's eyes gleamed red. She looked extremely angry.

"Well, I'll be . . ." said Rookery, impressed. "I've never seen anything like that before!"

Another cow drifted down—Cora—and then another and another, until all five of McLaughlin's vampire cows were floating in the air, facing the truck and lashing their tails like tense cats preparing to pounce.

Rookery stared back at them. Then his face split in a big grin. "Okay, cows," he said, putting the big truck into gear. "Prepare to be chopped meat!"

He stamped his foot on the accelerator, and with wheels spinning the truck lurched forward.

Rudolph quickly flew up into the air and out of sight.

"Hah!" said Rookery. "Coward!"

But the cows kept their position. Their eyes narrowed. Steam snorted from their nostrils.

Tony didn't want to look. The smash would be horrible. He gritted his teeth and looked anyway.

Rookery's truck was getting up to speed and the collision was imminent, when suddenly the cows lifted up into the air, one by one.

"Success!" crowed Rookery—too soon.

Mitsy released a big wet green cowpat as she flew over the truck. So did Cora. So did all of them. Tony could see the cowpats falling toward the truck, turning end over end.

Splat! Splat! Splat! Splat! Splat!

They rained into the windshield one after the other, completely covering it.

"Aaaargh!" yelled Rookery. He was going full speed, and he couldn't see a thing! At the next bend in the road, he failed to turn the corner and the truck smashed through a fence and into a big sign for the golf course and convention center. The impact knocked the steering wheel from Rookery's hands, and the truck rushed out of control over rough ground, bouncing and jiggling down a long slope toward the cliffs and the deep cold sea, its antivampire lights swinging wildly about the sky.

Tony stole a glance at Elizabeth's bonnet. In all

the bumping, it was slowly slipping toward him along the dashboard.

Rookery switched on the windshield wipers, but they simply smeared the mess around.

With a bump the truck ran over a bunker on the golf course. Before Rookery could regain control on the fairway, the truck was off into the rough again and heading farther down a steeper and steeper hill.

The bonnet fell off the dashboard into Tony's hands, and he grabbed it eagerly.

"Hey!" said Rookery, but he could do nothing just then, since he was fighting the controls of the runaway truck. He stood on the brake, but that had no effect.

Tony was rooted to his seat. He had the stone. What could he do now? He had no idea.

"The lights!" came a voice from above, shouting from far away.

Tony looked up.

"Shut off the lights!"

It was Rudolph! With Rookery's ultraviolet lights blazing, Rudolph couldn't get close.

Tony searched the control panels in front of him. X-ray, bat detector, stereo, smoke screen, multistake launch system, anchor, radio . . . UV lights!

He hit all the switches he could find, and all the bright lamps dimmed instantly.

Within seconds there was a loud clunk on the

cab roof and Rudolph's head appeared in the open hatch.

"Your hand!" he shouted. "Quick!"

Tony thrust his hand up, but Rookery, seeing that he was about to escape, grabbed his other hand, the one with the bonnet in it!

Rudolph tugged, and Rookery tugged. For one mad moment Tony felt that he was going to be torn apart, and Rookery and Rudolph would each be left with half of him!

Before that could happen, Tony gave up and dropped the wrapped bonnet onto Rookery's head. Rookery released his arm to make a grab for it—and Tony was free!

Rudolph pulled him out of the cab and the two friends sped up, up and away into the dark night sky. Rookery shook his fist after them.

"You got away, yes, but I've got the stone—"

There was a loud twang, and the sound of stretching wire. The cab jerked.

The windshield wipers cleared away some of the mess, and Rookery could see—cables? Somehow he had run into cables.

What was going on?

He looked up.

An enormous balloon was flying above him.

Bob and Dottie, Frederick and Freda, Gregory and Anna, all the vampire clan at the Gathering, and even Tony and Rudolph in the air with their

221

squadron of attack cows, had a grandstand view of what was happening.

Rookery's truck had gotten entangled in the lines holding Bob's blimp to the ground.

Everyone watched open-mouthed as the truck slowed and slowed but never quite came to a stop, and when it reached the cliff a few hundred yards from the Gathering it slowly—oh, so slowly—tipped over the edge.

There was no way back for Rookery.

The big blimp slowed his fall, but not by much, and in the slow motion of a nightmare, still clutching his useless steering wheel and still standing on the useless brakes, he fell slowly, majestically, headfirst down the cliff toward the waves crashing against the rocks below.

Chapter 34

"**H**ooray!" Gregory and Anna shouted together from the cliffside as they watched Rookery's ugly truck splash down into the water. Sparks flew as the electronics shorted out.

Freda looked up to the moon. "It won't be long now," she said.

"True," said Otto van Bleek, "but what has become of the Stone of Attamon?"

There was a murmur from the other gathered vampires. After all, they had also been on long hard journeys of their own for the previous three hundred years.

Despite still feeling unsteady, Frederick summoned up the energy to address the Gathering as the occasion deserved.

"After all of our wandering, all of our waiting, it's come to this. I do not have the stone."

"What!" "Why not!" "Disgraceful!" "Shame!" came from some of the older, bolder vampires.

"Stop that!" Gregory ordered, eyes blazing furiously.

"I am afraid I decided to leave our fate in the hands of two small boys," said Frederick. "Can you believe that? This is all my fault. I won't even ask for your forgiveness—I don't deserve it."

"Forgiveness?" said Freda. "For what? We have not lost. We have been brought together again, the entire clan. Even if we are trapped in this world of darkness for another three hundred years, it was worth it."

"Well, I don't know about that, old girl," said van Bleek. "Some of us are getting pretty cheesed off about the whole thing."

"It does sound like a rum do," agreed his wife, Eleanor.

"Perhaps, Frederick, your side of the family hasn't got what it takes, eh?" van Bleek suggested.

"Inviting mortals to our Gathering, I mean really . . ." said Eleanor, shuddering as she glanced at Bob and Dottie. "Mortals who aren't part of the snack service, anyway."

"Never mind all that," said Dottie hurriedly. "Where's Tony?"

Anna smiled up at her. "Tony is near," she said.

Dottie looked behind her, away from the cliff.

She could see no one coming up the road. "Where?"

Anna pointed into the sky. "There."

Bob and Dottie looked up, too. As Rudolph had predicted, they did not believe what they saw.

"Oh, my stars!" they said together, rubbing their eyes.

Tony was up there all right, out over the sea but coming in fast, smiling down at them. He waved as he crossed in front of the moon, grinning from ear to ear. Rudolph held his hand and smiled down at his own parents. And behind them, a herd of escorting vampire cows followed in perfect V-formation, as if they had been practicing air force maneuvers all their lives.

Tony and Rudolph banked and flew in over the cliff, then pulled up expertly and touched down on the grass softly.

The escort squadron of cows flew low over the crowd and thumped to less expert landings farther back. Mitsy sniffed at some grass and then turned away sadly. Grass no longer appealed to her. It was as though an old friend had become a stranger.

Now that Tony was on the ground, Bob and Dottie really believed it was him.

"Neat trick," said Bob.

"Tony!" shouted Dottie, but Tony just waved and ran up to Frederick. He held out his hand, opened it up.

"I think you're looking for this," he said proudly.

The Stone of Attamon gleamed in his palm, catching the rays of the moon and the comet and flashing with increasing power.

Frederick's eyes widened. "Three hundred years," he said, reaching for the jewel. "Thank you, Tony."

Reverently, Frederick clipped the stone back into its old familiar setting and held it high above his head so that its glow was visible to everyone.

"The stone is back!" he cried. "The Stone of Attamon is ours!"

All the vampires cheered and laughed and hugged one another. "Jolly good show!" "Top hole!" Those with hats threw them into the air.

"Now I can grow up and become your wife!" Anna squealed in Tony's ear.

Tony was not so sure about that; it was a scary idea.

"Tell her what you gave Rookery," said Rudolph, grinning.

At that very moment Rookery was finding out for himself. Still sitting in his truck cab, up to his chest in water, which rose higher as the truck slowly sank, sparks flying about from shorting electrics, he was still smiling.

He thought he still had the stone.

He unwrapped the bonnet to reveal his prize, only to find—a dead mouse? He stared at it.

In place of the Stone of Attamon lay Anna's dead mouse!

Rookery screamed and screamed and screamed, until all the sleeping birds and fishes nearby were forced to move away.

Chapter 35

The Grand Gathering of Sackville-Bagg vampires stood in a group, facing out to sea, eyes closed. Frederick and Freda, with Gregory, Anna, and Rudolph, stood at the front, in the lead, as befitted their role in finding the stone.

Bob and Dottie stood a respectful few yards back, with Tony, who was excitedly telling them all about his adventures.

They could only look at him in a daze as he explained flying vampire cows, coffins, the Stone of Attamon, and the various attempts of Rookery to catch them all.

"This ceremony," Tony said happily, "is just like the one in all those dreams I had. Except that in the dreams Rookery came riding in on a flaming cart."

"Rookery," said Bob, his jaw clenched. "Rookery, Rookery, Rookery. I wish I could get my hands on that guy!"

"Well, he's deep in the ocean now," said Dottie.

"But, Mom, Dad, do you know why I had the dreams? Because the stone was in my bedroom all the time. I wasn't crazy at all!"

Dottie mussed his hair. "Of course you weren't, hon."

Tony's features clouded briefly. "Uh, I do have a confession to make. We trashed my room. Pulled up some floorboards to find the stone."

"I don't think that matters now," said Dottie.

"And Rookery smashed some doors . . ."

"As long as you're safe," said Bob. "We can fix any door." He looked at the vampire gathering, shaking his head slowly as if he could not quite believe he was there watching. "Okay, Tony, so what happens now?"

"Sshh!" Tony urged.

The ceremony was starting.

"Now it is time," said Frederick.

Just as in Tony's dream, he lifted the complete amulet with the Stone of Attamon proudly set in the middle. The whole thing sparkled in the golden moonlight.

Frederick lined up the moon and the comet and the stone.

"Ab ovo," he intoned. *"Nil desperandum. Sine die."*

All the other vampires—there must have been twenty or more—harmonized in a high, wordless hum. The cows all mooed along, too, but not in the way normal cows moo. It was as though a small choir of deep basses had joined in. The sounds vibrated and merged with the singing vampires, rising and falling like the ocean currents and the wind rustling in the trees.

It was spooky. Tony felt the hairs on the back of his neck rise.

Then something really strange happened. Frederick and the vampires still had their eyes closed, so at first they did not see exactly what it was. Tony did. He could not remember this from his dream.

An enormous curved thing appeared over the edge of the cliff. It looked like a rising whale, or a planet, or maybe even a flying saucer.

Had a UFO come down to earth to take the vampires to a better life among the stars? Tony was beside himself with excitement.

The shape, dark and menacing, rose higher and higher, moving majestically. It was big and round, with quivering, rippling skin, and very soon it blocked the light of the moon.

Frederick opened his eyes, perplexed. This was not in the plan.

"Hey!" said Bob. "That's my blimp!"

It was. The name *McAshton* could be seen on its side. All the vampires opened their eyes and stared at the shape in front of them, as if the singing and the ceremony had hypnotized them. No one moved.

The blimp trailed some of its damaged cables.

One of them was taut, swinging.

And hanging from it, dripping, was Rookery, swinging like an angry pendulum.

"It's that guy!" Bob cried.

There was seaweed covering his head and murder in his eyes. Like a pirate boarding an ancient sailing ship with raised cutlass, Rookery roared and swung forward again. He held out his electric cross. It didn't work properly; full of water, it fizzed and sputtered.

Frederick stood there amazed, holding the amulet high above his head. He could not move.

Rookery aimed well with one leather boot and kicked the amulet hard. It flew out of Frederick's hands, flew high, spinning end over end. Other vampires, stirred from their daze, tried to grab it as it soared over their heads, but they could not.

Rookery reached the end of his swinging arc and jumped to the ground. He kept his eyes on the flying amulet, stepping back, one step, two . . . and he caught it!

All the vampires made a move toward him, but he kept them away with his fizzing cross. Reveling in his power, he pushed them back.

"Mom! Dad!" Tony yelled.

Bob flew into action. He ran toward Rookery, who recognized the danger.

"Another traitor!" he said, turning and running toward the cliff edge. Bob put on an extra burst of speed, reached out a hand, and grabbed Rookery's jacket, spinning him around. But Rookery was just too powerful, even running backward. He jerked his jacket out of Bob's hand.

Bob tripped and fell, landing with his face in a mud puddle.

"Ha!" said Rookery, triumphant on top of the cliff, surveying the cowering vampires below him. They could see his dark silhouette against the moon. The blimp drifted up high above him.

He raised the amulet with the Stone of Attamon and waved it in their faces.

"I have you now! I have you now!" he yelled, spit dribbling from his mouth. "Now it is straight to hell, my little fiends!"

Far out to sea, lightning crackled. The wind picked up. Power was surging through the atmosphere, expectant, electric.

Rookery turned to face the moon and recite his own dark chant in place of that of the vampires', only to find Dottie beside him. She had sneaked up unseen.

"Now, then, my dear," said Rookery, but it was too late for talking. Dottie wound up her right arm and punched him hard in the stomach. He bent over double, and she followed up with a real haymaker to the face. Rookery jerked back and, in the shock, threw the amulet high into the air.

Rookery stumbled, twisted, toppled backward over the edge, and went bouncing and crashing down the rocky face of the cliff, setting off a small avalanche of stones, which rattled down after him and followed him back into the sea.

Tony kept his eyes on the amulet as it flew up, spinning and glittering. Like a football player he ran away from the cliff, looking backward over his shoulder, timing its fall, watching it drop and drop—and fall into his hands.

"I got it!" he yelled, holding the amulet up so everyone could see. They were so far away.

At that moment the comet seem to touch the moon and the moon went a brilliant red. Bloodred.

"The ceremony, Tony!" shouted Frederick. "You must perform the ceremony!"

Tony stood there, uncertain what he should do.

"It's what we want, Tony!" Rudolph called to him. "Make a wish!"

Tony held the Stone of Attamon into the air, as he had seen Frederick do. He closed his eyes, trying to remember what Frederick said. *"Ab ovo . . ."* No, that had been done already.

What was he supposed to wish for? How was he supposed to wish it?

All he knew was that he really didn't want to lose his friends Rudolph and Anna.

At that very moment a blast of jagged red lightning shot out from the comet. It sparked across space and connected with the Stone of Attamon with such a blast of energy that Tony's hair stood on end and his glasses popped off his nose. The lightning twisted and turned, glowing and sizzling, like an enormous snake. But he felt no pain or shock; he was in the calm center of a storm.

The stone glowed brighter and brighter and brighter. Tony gripped it hard, but it got no hotter.

And then it seemed to explode like a fire-cracker! Still Tony held it tight. Smaller bolts of lightning forked off in every direction, twisting and crackling through the air.

They curved like long thin worms, arching up and over and then blasting through every single vampire on the cliff, including all the cows.

Rudolph was staring at Tony, who stared back at him.

Then Rudolph and Anna and Freda and all the other vampires sparked into flames that twisted into a tornado of furiously boiling smoke—and then they all just puffed out of existence, like the end of a dream.

Gone. They were all gone. Nothing and nobody was left, not even a cow. Just a few wisps of mist that soon blew away.

The moon was back to its normal color. The sky was dark and studded with stars. The waves crashed on the rocks far below, as they always did.

Tony stood there, horrified.

Bob and Dottie walked up to him and put their hands on his shoulders.

"What did you wish for, son?" Bob asked, kindly.

But Tony, in shock, could not say. He stood there, tears in his eyes, staring out to sea.

What had he done? Had he done Rookery's work for him and condemned his friends to some awful fate?

"Hello there, Thompson," came a voice from a hundred yards away. It was Lord McAshton. "Those aristocratic so–called friends of yours, they're vampires! Beware! They're vampires!"

"Well," said Dottie, under her breath. "I guess he's right about that."

"I forgot to tell you," said Tony, his eyes cold, "that Lord McAshton helped Rookery lock me in a coffin."

"*What!*"

"Did he, now," said Bob, his mouth in a tight smile. "Hey, buster," he shouted, "I've got a couple of bones to pick with you." He strode off.

McAshton turned and ran for his Bentley.

Out to sea, there were a few bubbles.

Suddenly a shape burst from the depths—

235

Rookery, gasping for air. He pulled on a toggle and one of his inflatable devices opened with a sound like a popped balloon.

It was a small lifeboat. Rookery struggled into it and lay there like a stranded fish, spluttering and dripping water.

Picked up by the current, the lifeboat drifted out to sea, into the night. Every now and then, when Rookery had breath, he cursed the day he had met Tony Thompson.

Chapter 36

Tony was inconsolable for days after the Gathering, moping around at home and miserable at school, kicking himself for his mistake.

Luckily for him, no one dared to tease him anymore. His mom and dad, of course, knew everything, although they still could not really believe what they had seen with their own eyes.

Everyone at school—indeed, everyone in the village, including Nigel and Flint and Mr. Boggins, the teacher—had seen the moon turn bright red, just as Tony had predicted. The event was in all the newspapers. People treated him with a new respect, as if they knew he had been endowed with strange powers.

Mr. Boggins, of course, had even seen the vampire bats though his telescope, flying in for the Gathering. He suspected there was a connection, but wisely for his career he did not ask Tony about it or mention it to anyone else. But he never made fun of Tony again, and he made sure no one else did, either.

After school one day, Tony did what he did every day now. He got on his bike and rode around the village and its outskirts, pedaling hard. He knew that if he just sat at home, staring out of the window, he would start to believe he really had gone crazy. Rudolph in the fireplace! Jumping out of the window with Rookery! Flying through the air! Bouncing on the blimp!

Ridiculous!

So he cycled around, looking again at the various places where he remembered having adventures, trying to prove to himself that it had really happened.

He rode to McAshton Manor. Lord McAshton himself had disappeared, gone abroad suddenly, and some people in the village thought he would never come back. Even Nigel and Flint didn't know where he was. In his absence, Bob had been appointed chief executive of the golf course and convention center project, which was a nice promotion.

The blimp was back at the manor, but it was not flying. It had been found farther down the coast, tattered and torn. That was evidence for

Tony that what he remembered had really happened, though most people thought the blimp had just blown away. Tony liked to look at it every day and remember bouncing on top of it with Rudolph.

And every day he visited the old McAshton mausoleum behind the manor. The door was still open, hanging on its broken hinges, where McAshton had left it as he fled after Rookery.

Somehow Tony didn't feel like going down into the depths and walking along the tunnel. He didn't want to see Von and Elizabeth's tomb either. All that had been easier to do with Rudolph and Anna.

Just outside the wall of the old ruined church, Rookery's drill holes were still dotted about, looking more like big pancakes now, after some rain.

Tony leaned his bike against the church wall and wandered into the cemetery, walking among the headstones in the sunlight. Here was where he had first met Rudolph's family. Frederick and Freda had swooped down there. Here was where he had his first encounter with Gregory.

He looked down the hole he had fallen into when Rookery was chasing him, and Rudolph had saved him.

And a little farther away he could see the deep tire tracks from Rookery's truck. As he stood there, he thought he could hear the deep, throaty rumble of Rookery's truck engine vibrating through the air.

Wait a minute. That was a real engine noise coming from the grounds of the rectory next door. Tony scrambled up the remains of a ruined wall and knelt down. He pushed aside the branches of an overgrown bush.

A hundred yards away across the lawns a big moving truck was parked in the driveway of the rectory. The driver—or someone in overalls, anyway—pulled the For Sale sign out of the ground.

It looked as though the place had been sold. No one in the village knew what had happened to the caretaker, who'd been house-sitting. Obviously his job was finished. Tony idly wondered who was moving in.

Five black-and-white cows walked sedately around the corner of the big house and munched contentedly on the grass. That was odd, Tony thought. Cows? He smiled, wishing them luck. They sure wouldn't be allowed to do that for long.

He was just beginning to think the cows looked familiar when he was distracted by a Land Rover. It weaved up the driveway, kicking up dust. For a second Tony thought it was his mom and dad, but the car was the wrong color and was moving erratically, almost as though the driver had never operated it before.

The Land Rover jerked to a halt in front of the house, then jumped forward and stalled.

A skinny man, about as tall as Frederick, got out of the driver's side, and a woman who looked a bit like Freda got out of the passenger seat. The back doors opened and three kids got out. Good, thought Tony. Give someone else the responsibility of being the new kids in town.

They looked familiar, too. A teenage boy, another boy a little older than Tony who looked a lot like Rudolph, and a girl who looked like Anna.

Wait a minute. That *was* Gregory! It *was* them! All of them! The whole family was back, and even the cows!

They were walking about in the sunlight, as Rudolph had always wanted! Tony slapped his head with the palm of his hand. So that was how his wish had come true.

The family was yawning and stretching. Tony didn't wait any longer.

"Hey!" he shouted, leaping over the wall. "Hey, it's me! Rudolph! Anna!"

They heard him, but it was as though they couldn't see him. Their heads turned this way and that, trying to pin him down.

He ran toward them. The boy who looked like Gregory saw him when he was halfway across the lawn, and pointed to him. All the others looked over as well, their heads moving a little oddly. The girl who looked like Anna knelt to pick a bright red flower.

Tony slowed down, feeling foolish. They didn't recognize him. It couldn't be them. Whoever it was, they all looked very pale and wan, and they moved slowly, as if they had been on a very long journey and were half asleep.

Maybe, thought Tony, the sunlight was too bright. That would account for the driving, of course.

But it sure looked like them. The closer he got, the more sure Tony became.

"It's me, Tony," he said again, hopefully.

Nothing. They all just stared at him, open-mouthed, as if he was invisible.

Then he thought of Anna's advice: If you need me, just whistle.

Okay, give it a try. He formed his lips into a round shape and blew. The sound was wet and weedy and nothing like a whistle. Just the way his whistles always sounded. Dribbly.

But the Girl Who Looked Like Anna smiled and whispered to the Boy Who Looked Like Rudolph. He smiled, too, and a look of understanding crossed his face, what little of it Tony could see.

The two walked toward Tony, and they all met in the middle of the lawn and shook hands.

The five black-and-white cows mooed.

Soon Farmer McLaughlin would be told and would come to collect them and take them home.

Unknown to everyone, down in the gloomy basement of the rectory a dark shape lay slumbering on a slab.

The caretaker, still in the village after all, still carrying the scars of Gregory's fang marks in his neck.

He lay there through the heat of the day, earplugs jammed in his ears.

But when the night came, he would wake again.

It was the way of his kind.

He would wake, and he would need something to drink!

About the Authors

Angela Sommer-Bodenburg was born in Reinbek, near Hamburg, Germany. She attended the University of Hamburg and taught first- to fourth-graders in Hamburg for twelve years. Since 1984 she has been a freelance writer and a painter. To date, more than forty of her books have been published, including poetry, picture books, novels, and the eighteen-volume series The Little Vampire. Her books have been translated into thirty languages and have sold more than ten million copies.

Many of Angela Sommer-Bodenburg's books have been adapted in many countries for radio, stage play, and musical productions; book readings on audio tape; dramatized plays on audio tape; and in Braille. The Little Vampire series has been adapted into two major thirteen-part European television series (first released in 1985 and again in 1993), which have been broadcast throughout Europe and Canada.

Angela Sommer-Bodenburg moved to the United States in 1992. She lives and works in Southern California with her husband and business manager, Burghardt, and their Spanish mastiff, Hanna. To find out more about Angela Sommer-Bodenburg, visit her Web site, www.AngelaSommer-Bodenburg.com.

Nicholas Waller was born in 1958 in Beirut, Lebanon. He worked in the publishing business until 1996, when he chose to give it up to test the creative waters. He started writing short stories and scripts, and hanging around on film sets, where he is fast becoming an expert in the whole moviemaking creative process. He has had several short stories published, and his first full screenplay, a biopic of Russian cosmonaut Yuri Gagarin, is set to go into production in 2001.